It Came Upon Christmas Eve

(A book of short stories for Christmas)

By

S.R. Kerr

Contents

Chapter 1

THE CHILDREN
OF MUFFBERRY GRUFF

The window of a room in a B&B looked down into the long, slim, vertical windows of the old school. Its myriad of rooms and tarmac playground had long been deserted. A FOR SALE sign hung on its railings. Would it be converted into luxury flats or would its rooms be taken over by up-and-coming private enterprises where each business was a room? The detached Edwardian houses that surrounded it crouched in their modest cosiness behind hedges and low walls that lined the main road. An early afternoon twilight air hovered over the place as the wind blew the trees and bushes, keeping them from sleep under the grey skies of late December. It had seemed a sensible arrangement to book a B&B over Christmas, now that both of my parents and most of my aunts and uncles had passed on. They appeared now only in memories and in recollections of certain words and sentences that they had once uttered during their earthly sojourn.

* * *

No one knew exactly how the place had acquired its somewhat nonsensical name. There were various obscure myths concerning its origins. The most credible seemed to be that a cottage stood next to a mulberry tree on a stream that locals called the Gruff, a variation of an old Saxon word. Around the mid-eighteenth century, but then nobody is really certain of the exact date., a young widow inhabited the cottage. She arrived at the property shortly after the death of her husband, a farmer. With ten hungry mouths to feed, she began to make muffs for the ladies of the area to wear, to keep their hands free from the cold. Each winter, she was inundated with requests for muffs, and word of their high quality spread far beyond the neighbourhood. The widow became a local celebrity and lived to a ripe old age. Muffs from Mulberry on the Gruff soon became corrupted to Muffberry Gruff, which was the name that the area became known by, years after the old widow's death and long after both the mulberry tree had disappeared and the stream had been built over. In the 1880s, a well-off ne'er-do-well of an industrialist, who owned a mansion on the site that bore the name Muffberry Gruff, gifted the building to the local council on the condition that it be used as a school. That was what it became to generations of local children in town ... including me. I had graced its large portal fifty-three years ago, when it still reflected the original aspects of its Victorian

utilitarianism, so omnipresent in the spartan educational system of its day. Utilitarianism is recorded in the Charles Dickens novel *Hard Times* and embodied in its protagonist, Mr Gradgrind, whose sole preoccupation is facts, facts, and cold facts. Mr Gradgrind's ghost still seemingly haunted our present society, where the accumulation of figures and facts to accelerate finances had taken over from sentimentality, which lay dilapidated and unkempt in the far corner of our modern existence.

* * *

The breakfast tables in the guest house were set for only two people. The white linen napkins weaved themselves, uninvited, through the hoops of slim silver bands that lay horizontally on floral-rimmed yellow side plates. A large overgrown aspidistra sprawled its verdancy over a highly polished, rotund bowl, patterned in shades of light and deep blue. A short grey-haired woman in her seventies walked into the deep, warm, wintery shades of the breakfast room. She wore jeans, a cherry mohair top, and no makeup, and she smiled through a plain, long face. Her grey hair was somewhat thin in parts. Her eyes reflected a Southern European component in her genealogy and she spoke in an unashamedly local dialect, free of all pretensions. A nervous yet undetectable ray of low self-esteem hid just beneath her skin. She filled a square glass tumbler with the orange juice that sat on the wooden ledge, next to the aspidistra. The woman put her hand inside a brown leather shoulder bag and took out two white plastic containers, then emptied two pills from each onto a side plate. As I looked over to the window, shrouded in a crocheted curtain, the woman moved her lips genteelly. "Morning!" she said

"Morning!" I replied cheerfully.

"Spending Christmas here, are you?" she enquired.

"Yes, I`m here right through till January 2ⁿᵈ."

"I`m here only until the 27ᵗʰ. Then I go back."

"And where`s back?" I asked.

"Well, I go back to Cyprus. That's home to me, for the moment."

"So, where are you from originally?"

"I`m from here. I used to live on Montague Road."

"Oh, really? Why, I used to live two minutes from there on Aragon Street."

"Oh? What a coincidence!" she said as she spread some butter onto her toast.

Mrs Gillfillan, the host, entered the room, carrying a bacon sandwich in her left hand and a plate of poached eggs in her right.

"Is everything alright?" she asked.

We both returned a positive reply; nothing to complain about. Content at our response, Mrs Gillfillan clasped her hands together and exited the room, then descended the back steps in the hallway that led to the small kitchen in the basement.

"Are you visiting family?" the woman enquired cautiously, after a few seconds of silence.

"Indeed I am. I have a brother and an aunt who live not too far from here. They both live in somewhat cramped accommodation, so I decided it would be best if I booked in here for this week."

"Yes, I have a sister-in-law who still lives on Montague Road. She`s getting on now and I don`t like to impose. This is the first time I`ve stayed at the Aberlea. Three years ago and one year before that, I booked into the Rosebush Guest House. I always found it very acceptable but they closed last year. The owners, an ex-sea captain and his wife, both retired from the hospitality business."

The bacon was just a tinge underdone. Maybe I should have asked for it to be grilled until crisp. I sipped at my warm coffee.

"Did you know David Ives?"

"David Ives?"

"Yes, he lived on Montague Road."

"I can`t say I do. What number?"

"I can`t recall the number but he lived in the third house after the phone box. He was in my class at school. Do you remember old Mrs Feathery who always used to sit on her window sill on sunny days?"

"No, I can`t say I do. You see, I was always busy working and didn`t have that much contact with the neighbours."

"And then there was that very glamorous woman who was crowned Miss Sandy Beach 1967 ... remember? She went on to come in second at the Miss United Kingdom contest. Let`s see, her name was ... er ... Mae."

The old woman`s face lit up. She laughed loudly and smiled.

"Mae Laurence, Miss Sandy Beach 1967! Why, that was me!"

Through the ageing face and thinning grey hair, I suddenly recognised her. "Mae Laurence, of course. Mae, it`s you!"

She looked at my face as if checking each of my features. Then, shaking her head, she said, "I`m really sorry but I can't remember you."

"Well, it was a long time ago. I used to come to your house when I was in primary school. I was friendly with your two sons."

"What`s your name?"

"I`m Robert, Robert Baxter."

"Baxter? Baxter? No, I'm sorry but as you say, it's a long time ago."

"I remember you used to be married to the football player Billy Lake, didn't you?"

"Yes, married for fifteen years but we divorced some time ago now."

"I remember you well. You were the chicest, most glamorous couple in town."

Mae laughed heartily. "Were we?" she asked with an air of feigned surprise.

"You were both on TV quite often, as well."

"Yes, my ex-husband more than me but I remember when I came in second at the Miss United Kingdom beauty contest extremely well. My photo was in all the papers. It's years ago but it's still as clear as day to me. I felt like a real celeb. Of course, times have changed, as have society's values. Beauty contests no longer have any merit or importance. I suppose, now, I don't really approve of them either, yet I would be a liar if I said that I wasn't euphoric at the time."

A calm, content nostalgia seemed to rest comfortably on her brow and all around us at the Aberlea Guest House, where, in a potluck of coincidence, both of us were seeking an elusive Christmas – a Christmas as I had once experienced. We had both returned here to our hometown trying desperately hard to find it and for it to never leave our grasp.

* * *

After visiting my aunt on the afternoon of December 23rd, I walked along the main road that cut through town and on which the Aberlea was situated. Visitors entered and departed from the town on this road, which was now rich in traffic lights and Belisha beacons – fairly new additions to the scene. I had walked down this very same road as a child when it had been devoid of such highway attractions. It had been an annual tradition of mine, on the early evening of the 23rd, to walk along the residential area of the road and admire the host of large, bedecked Christmas trees illuminated by strands of fairy lights beneath veils of angel hair. I would stand outside each splendored bay window in the melange of diverse Victorian edifices, populated by the comfortably well-off, and simply stand in awe as the waves of peak-time traffic made their way from the workplace to the home. Muffberry Gruff Primary School stood at the far end of the buildings, on the left-hand side just next to the entrance of the Aberlea, whose grounds were shrouded from view by high hedges of prickly holly. The residents of the old Victorian buildings, whom I had been familiar with as a boy, had almost all gone. The old had passed on and their offspring had all moved to other parts of the country. New faces, mostly from out of town, had replaced them, yet the trees in their splendour still reappeared year after year. I stopped for a short moment to savour the treasure chest of memories that beckoned me from behind the tall iron railings. The arched entrance to the playground was enshrined behind railings with the name Muffberry Gruff carved in gold letters, crowning its somewhat regal appearance. In the dark, unlit corner where it stood, it was barely visible to the eye. I peered sentimentally through the railings until my cheeks rested on the iron and my nose protruded through the space between them. Lights from passing cars unexpectedly illuminated me for a few seconds, then left me in darkness again as if propelling me briefly into the limelight of fame and then suddenly leaving me as a fallen star. Through the darkness, I could see the outline of the gables and the curved long windows through which I had drooled and daydreamed while writing essays on lethargic Friday afternoons in the early 1960s. The impolite traffic broke the silence and its intermittent light lit up the rows of apple trees that sat on a grassy bank at the rear of the playground. I could still hear old Miss Sangster sternly telling us that the apples did not belong to the pupils and that it was strictly forbidden to eat them. Miss Sangster's wooden ruler had inflicted so much pain on the tips of my fingers but she was always fair and tried hard to instil morals into us sometimes unruly children. I walked farther round the railings that lined the part of the playground on the main road and turned off into the quiet residential side street where there were two smaller entrances: one with "BOYS" engraved above it and one with "GIRLS." As I walked closer to the grassy bank, where stood the apple trees, I could hear the faint sound of high-pitched children's voices punctuated by impish laughter. Through the darkness, I could just about see the outline of a few small figures among the trees. As I walked back onto the main road, I peered again through the railings and clearly saw a group of children running happily towards me. I counted them, ten in all: six boys and four girls. The boys' hair was clipped, short, and spiky while the girls sported ringlets. I noticed that the boys all wore tank tops and shorts. Some of the shorts were rather long and came past their knees. The girls wore bows in their ringlets and scarves around their necks. I could not help but take note of the patches and areas of their clothes that had been stitched, as if they had been well-used hand-me-downs. A most definite aroma of carbolic soap exuded from them as they giggled and smiled in an outgoing, friendly manner. I would have put their ages at between ten and twelve. The tallest of the boys asked me where I was from. He peered through the lenses of rounded, cheaply made National Health glasses, curiously, as if I were some sort of alien. One of the little girls did a hop-scotch routine, hitting the tarmac of the playground with the soles of her shoes. She seemed a happy, content little thing. "She`s my sister," said the tallest of the boys. "Aren`t you, Helen?"

The little lass giggled. "Yes, he`s Bill and I`m his sister."

"And is he a good brother?" I asked, tongue in cheek.

"No, he`s lazy. He lies in bed till late. He never helps Mum to wash up and he eats all my sweets."

"No I don`t," replied her brother.

His sister began to laugh. "Yes, you do. You know you do," she said. Then, looking up at my face, she added,

"But he`s very kind as well."

"I`m glad to hear that," I said with a smile.

"We`ve never seen you pass this way before," said a small, red, curly-haired boy with a navy tank top.

"I don`t live here now. I live in London."

"Oooh, London!" they all said in unison, swooning in disbelief.

"But that`s a huge city," said another small girl with a missing front tooth.

"Yes," said the tallest boy. "It`s got hundreds and hundreds of people."

"Yes, it has," I said. "Even more than that."

"Imagine," said the smallest of the girls, who clutched a worn, cloth doll.

"But I used to go to school here at Muffberry Gruff, the same as you."

The children began to laugh.

"Imagine," said the small girl who had been doing the hopscotch routine. "You, a child just the same as us."

"Hard to believe, I know," I said, "But I can assure you, I was once a child, really!"

"How old are you now?" asked a boy with cropped hair. He sported a Rupert Bear badge on his jumper. "You must be thirty or something now."

"Oh, I`m a lot older than that," I said, laughing.

They stared at me, somewhat bemused.

"What are you all doing out in the dark of early evening?" I enquired.

A boy who looked like the youngest of the group replied. "We`ve come here to play amongst the apple trees."

"But don`t your parents mind?" I asked.

"No, not at all. They know that we`re safe."

"Well, I`m glad to hear that," I said, not totally convinced.

"Yes, safe we are. Safe as houses," said a boy with extra spiky hair that seemed to stand on end.

The eldest boy endorsed him. "Yes, safe we are. Safe as houses," he echoed.

One of the group articulated an elfin-like giggle. Then, in a potage of "bye-byes" and "cheerios," they ran and skipped back towards the grassy bank and the row of apple trees. Suddenly, they were consumed by the darkness of the late December afternoon and were gone.

Once again, the playground of Muffberry Gruff Primary was empty and still. Its graven facade, which even yet reflected the pain of Miss Sangster's ruler, looked down at me in its unique fusion of strict discipline, tempered by a touch of kindness and compassion. A few passing vehicles cajoled the playground into a spotlight and then it faded back into the shyness of eventide.

I put my key into the front door of the guest house and opened the warmth and light that its promises held. The staircase spiralled in front of me, clad in its deep, dark red carpet as the doors at its base opened and invited me into the unveiled, snug refuge of the wood-panelled drawing room, itself fitted in a thick, dark blue shag pile carpet topped with Persian rugs. Mae sat on the burgundy leather sofa in front of the heavy teak mantelpiece. She was busy writing a letter. CDs were scattered across the cushions on the sofa. I observed that they were all by artists particular to the 1960s: The Tremeloes, Manfred Mann, Sandie Shaw, Cilla Black, and P J Proby. She commented on my interest as I inspected their sleeves.

"I bought a whole batch of them today. A little Christmas treat for myself. What memories all these songs hold for me. They are all proper artists as well, not like that talentless mob that passes for pop singers these days."

"Well, the 60s was the defining decade for pop, wasn't it?"

"Indeed, they were and I'm proud and glad that I was a child of the 60s."

"Well, it was very much your decade, wasn't it? I mean, Miss Sandy Beach 1967, face in all the tabloids, TV appearance on Miss United Kingdom, Married to a rising star of football. It sounds all so jet set to me."

Mae laughed and gave my arm a gentle slap in jest.

"Oh, you make me feel as if I were some sort of star."

"Well, I suppose you were. You and your husband, the Liz Taylor and Richard Burton of Montague Road. The local Posh and Becks of your day."

"Oh, happy days, happy days," she said in response. The expression in her eyes rested on a comfy cushion of nostalgia, far away from the moment. "It`s such a pity they couldn`t have gone on forever. All part of a different era mind, I suppose. There were fewer opportunities for a woman back then. I mean, nowadays most sensible girls would rather do a degree in law or start a business than enter a beauty pageant."

Mrs Gillfillan, the guest house proprietor, came into the room.

"I do hope you are both comfortable here. If there`s anything I can do for you, don`t be afraid to give me a shout," she said as she retrieved a dirty cup from the coffee table. "Remember and fill in the menu if you want to have an evening meal tomorrow."

"Oh, yes, Mrs Gillfillan," said Mae. "I`m certainly going to have dinner here tomorrow. I`m meeting an old school friend for coffee in the afternoon and I`ll be spending Christmas Day at my sister-in-law's but I can confirm that I`ll be dining here tomorrow."

"Well, there`s a choice of fish pie or macaroni cheese for dinner but you can sort that out later when you tick off your choice on the menu that I left in your room."

"Of course, no bother, Mrs Gillfillan," said Mae.

"I`m going to the watchnight service tomorrow at the church across the road. If you're going to be alone, maybe you might like to come with me. I`ll be going on my own. Mr Gillfillan's too advanced in years to stay up late."

Mae`s eyes lit up. Then, as if she had been told off, she changed her expression in reply to the offer.

"Yes, that would be pleasant but I ... er ... prefer to spend Christmas Eve warm and comfortable in my room. But thanks anyway."

"I just didn`t want you to feel lonely, that`s all," said Mrs Gillfillan.

I broke into the conversation with a chain of coughs.

"Are you alright?" enquired Mrs Gillfillan.

"Yes, I'm fine but I went out without my scarf and I think I may have caught a chill."

"Oh, maybe you're coming down with something," said Mae.

"Yes, you might be," said Mrs Gillfillan. "Can I get you a drink?"

"No, I'm sure I'll be alright," I said.

Mae looked at me with some empathy. "Oh, but you don't want to be ill over Christmas, do you?"

"Would you like a hot toddy?" asked Mrs Gillfillan.

"Oh, alright then. That would be nice," I said.

"I'll prepare that right now, with pleasure," said Mrs Gillfillan as she nodded. Then she headed out of the inviting drawing room and waltzed her way briskly towards the kitchen in the basement.

The Gillfillans had owned the Aberlea Guest House since 1978. It had, in its day, been a thriving little enterprise that burst with the bustle of enthusiastic tourists from as far as Newcastle, Glasgow, and Leeds, bent on a fortnight of diversion by the sea, far from the grime of their everyday inner-city lives and the foul city air. As the Gillfillans aged with the ever-changing seasons that accumulated over years, they made a small fortune from their lucrative little venture. The day, however, came when they decided to limit the number of guests to only a handful and then merely a trickle at designated times of the year. There were now never more than two, and at the very most three, guests in residence over a few weeks in the summer and at Christmas and New Year. As the Gillfillans had become elderly, they began to see the guest house as something that surpassed profit and that now, in their old age, was their vocation. Their aim was to dote on their guests and make sure that their stay at the Aberlea was as enjoyable and comfortable as possible. Mr Gillfillan, who had once played a very active part in the running of the place, including marketing, cooking, and chauffeuring guests to the station, was now well into his eighties and rarely left their private flat at the top of the stairs. There were exceptions to this when, in the summer months, he would sit in the garden and watch the world go by and the few guests come and go.

The clock in the drawing room ticked into the peace of the winter's s evening. After a break of 15 minutes, Mrs Gillfillan returned with the hot toddy, which she presented to me in a thick, tall glass. She was just about to exit the room again when, almost as an afterthought, she turned round and fixed her gaze on Mae.

"Oh, I almost forgot. Can I get you anything? A small sherry, perhaps?

"No," said Mae abruptly. Then she gave a barely audible laugh. "No, thank you," she said as if correcting her bad-mannered abruptness. "That's very kind of you but no thanks."

I looked at Mae and her movements as she jerked nervously. How plain and devoid of glamour she appeared now in comparison to what I remembered her to be. She now also came over as very nervous and unsure of herself. I recalled how all the women on Aragon Street commented on her fashionable wardrobe and natural beauty. Often in vain attempts, they tried to emulate her. The male population of the street envied her husband for being married to one so stunningly beautiful as she was then, with her hazel eyes and long black hair making her reminiscent of Bizet's Carmen.

I retired to my room. There, I sank into the comfort of an easy chair and pressed the TV's remote control. Frank Capra's classic Christmas offering "It's a Wonderful Life" flashed up on the flat screen. I had, of course, viewed this on a myriad of occasions, yet it was a film I never tired of even though I knew the plot of the 1940s melodrama like the palm of my hand.

Slowly, I felt the comforting warmth of the hot toddy. Mrs Gillfillan had certainly put in plenty of whisky, and I could taste a trace of honey, which she had substituted for sugar. Soon, I fell into a state of complete relaxation as I watched James Stewart's escapades on a snowy Christmas Eve in his small provincial town and his encounter with his guardian angel. After the credits of the film rolled on the screen, I could feel myself beginning to doze off. I forcibly pulled my consciousness together and arose from the armchair. Having then decided it was time to retire, I walked over to the window that looked out onto the playground of Muffberry Gruff and began to close the curtains. As I looked down below, I could see ten distinct figures laughing and playing on its grounds. It was the group of children with whom I had spoken to earlier. *But look at the time!* It was now becoming very late. *What sort of parents would allow their children out to play at this time of night, school holidays or not?* I couldn't help but notice how some of the children's clothes had been sewn and patched as if their parents could not afford to buy new ones. I watched them play for a few seconds and I wondered where they lived. The town, luckily, still had a low crime rate compared to other places, yet, at the same time, it was hardly crime-free and one heard such awful stories on the news these days. I closed the thick curtains on the children of Muffberry Gruff as they continued to play and I looked forward to a good night's sleep.

* * *

Having breakfasted at 9 a.m., I decided to go into town to buy some Christmas presents for my aunt and brother's family. To embark on Christmas shopping on Christmas Eve was a hazardous experience, especially when one had no idea what to buy. A book for my aunt? A fur headband? A large box of Belgian chocolates? And what about my brother? Another football top? A CD? Grumpy, stressed-out Christmas shoppers moaned, groaned, and pushed each other in overcrowded shops, all in the name of peace on earth.

I wandered from shop to store in dithering indecisiveness, through one door and another until I was punch-drunk on prospective Christmas gifts. The Salvation Army provided a Christmas cabaret of well-loved carols in the High Street as mid-morning turned into early afternoon and presents had still not been purchased. I thought it best to indulge in a cappuccino and contemplate over its froth. Massari's Tea Rooms, which had provided generations with ham sandwiches, tea, coffee, and scones, had now been turned into a Cafe Costa branch but it was still a shelter from the tidal wave of shoppers. The scrumptious homebaked cakes that had once made Massari's so special had been replaced by mass-produced biscuits and cakes in cellophane packets. I drank the cappuccino, which proved to be food for thought and produced several fruitful ideas on the buying of presents. By 2.30 p.m., my mission had been accomplished.

I did not take the direct route back to the guest house but instead walked past the picturesque fisherman's cottages by the harbour and into Aragon Street, where I had once lived. Much had changed since I last played in its precincts. While the rest of Sandy Beach had gone upwardly mobile, Aragon Street had gone downhill. The once well-kept terraced houses were now run down, their windows dirty and displaying unkempt interiors, while the once dutifully maintained gardens and doorsteps were now overgrown and crumbling. Broken TV sets and fridges populated the pavement whose flagstones had once glowed and been carefully preserved. At the end of the street, Annie and Jack Petrie's corner shop had provided the area with various basics, as well as sweets and newspapers. It was now a Tesco Express. It had been many years since my last visit to Aragon Street and I now thought it was perhaps best not to return. Instead, I would preserve the place in my museum of memories, as I had once remembered it to be.

I turned the corner at the end of the street, just next to Tesco Express, which opened onto the promenade that ran parallel to the beach. The afternoon was bleak. From the dull and overcast sky, the sound of seagulls descended. I felt a definite chill in the air as I strolled past the deep, beige, sandy dunes and the last house in town. The lights from its Christmas tree shone out onto the sea like some sort of lighthouse as Christmas crept closer to the shore.

* * *

Mrs Gillfillan was hacking at a thick holly bush with a pair of secateurs as I opened the gate of the Aberlea's garden.

"I just thought I'd fill the house with a bit more festive greenery before the big day," she said as she pressed her weight on the rather uncooperative secateurs. A leopard skin jacket that was now fit only for gardening and a pair of tight leather gloves kept out the cold. It was indeed becoming colder and colder as the day went on. It would be a frosty night, as predicted. The darkness of the eventide made a gradual appearance from the window of my room. I looked down onto the playground of Muffberry Gruff Primary and the silhouettes of the mansions built on the hill behind it. They were replicas of French chateaux that had been constructed by the wealthy pioneers of the industrial revolution in the confusing and changing days of the late eighteenth century – symbols of a new order that challenged the old aristocratic, land-owning class. Muffberry Gruff was a byword for finesse in the town whose once grandiose residences had now been mostly divided into flats. In the 1960s, the economic boom saw the extensive gardens of the mansions sold off and bought by those who had never had it so good, who constructed neat little bungalows on the grounds. They were owned by a generation whose salaries had ballooned and for whom disposable income had become a reality. It was a generation and an era to which Mae had belonged. I could hear the sounds of the 1960s coming from her door as I passed. She was obviously enraptured by the CDs that she had bought the previous day. The recordings meant so much to her. In their notes, she relived her youth and dusted off her happy memories.

I had not yet read the newspapers, so I thought it a good idea to return downstairs to the drawing room and browse the selection of dailies on display there. In sharp contrast to the sounds of the 1960s that came from Mae`s room upstairs, the haunting, quasi-spiritual sound of Bing Crosby`s rendition of Adeste Fidelis drifted tunefully up to the drawing room`s high ceiling.

The Gillfillans' black Persian cat made a stately entrance into the arena, as if it were some Eastern monarch, wrapped in a winter robe of elegant dark fur.

"That`s Nanotchka, our ageing family pet," said Mrs Gillfillan. A smirk came over her face. "She`s getting on now but when she was in her prime, she was a star beauty. Yes, won many a prize in her day. She won Cat of the Year at the Colliston Annual Cat Show."

"A bit like Mae, then," I stated with a hint of a suppressed snigger.

Mrs Gillfillan looked confused. "What do you mean?"

"Well, Mae in her heyday was a beauty queen. Miss Sandy Beach 1967 and runner-up at the Miss United Kingdom contest, in the days when all that meant something."

"Fancy that!" she said. "I didn't know."

As if we had mentioned the devil himself, Mae entered the room, aware that we had been speaking about her. She sat down sheepishly, unsure of her place in our opinions. There followed a minute of sheer silence. Mrs Gillfillan spoke to break it.

"Er ... Another guest will be joining you for breakfast on Christmas Day, a Mr. Weston. He comes over from Glasgow every Christmas Eve, spends it with his mother and stays here. Then, after breakfast on Christmas Day, he takes his mother back to Glasgow. It's a long way to spend Christmas Day and Boxing Day with his family there. One year we were snowed in till the 28th. It doesn't look as if we're going to get thick snow and freezing temperatures this year."

"It's certainly not snowing but hasn't the temperature dropped considerably today?" asked Mae.

"Well, we'll just have to be like Bing Crosby," I said.

"In what way?" asked Mae.

"Well, we'll just have to dream about it. Dream about a white Christmas."

"I'm not so fond of snow," said Mrs Gillfillan." I wouldn't object to Christmas in Australia. I could very well live with that. I love the heat."

"Oh, no!" said Mae in disagreement. "I live in Cyprus. Believe me, by the time November comes, you're sick of the sun. Snow would be very welcome in my opinion."

"Oh, I can't think of anything more akin to heaven than a Christmas in Cyprus," responded Mrs Gillfillan.

"I've had enough mild, sunny, Christmases in Cyprus to last me a lifetime. I want to experience again the crisp cold of a white Christmas here," said Mae just as Nanotchka ran out of the room.

Mrs Gillfillan took note and said, "Time for Moggie's tea." She made her way down to the kitchen in the basement. After a few seconds had lapsed, her head reappeared briefly through the open door. "Care for a Buck's Fizz tomorrow with breakfast?"

I responded promptly, "Oh, yes, please!"

"Er ... no ... no ... not for me, thanks," said Mae. Her serious expression gave way to a polite smile.

Bing Crosby, who was my uncle's favourite singer, proceeded to croon from the grave, in total harmony with the tunes from yesteryear. He reminded me of my headmaster at Muffberry Gruff Primary, Mr Wilson, who remained head long after retirement age. "Bing Crosby was a crooner," he once told me. "Not only a crooner but my own favourite singer."

Crosby continued to entertain both Mae and myself on that particular Christmas Eve with renditions of God Rest You Merry Gentlemen, I'll Be Home for Christmas, Christmas in Killarney, and a host of other favourites from the 1930s and 1940s – an era that had passed and seemed so long gone, just as one day our own would be.

The drawing room soon filled with an ambiance that was particular to Christmas Eve. Mae sang along to the Crosby songs under her breath

"So you don't miss Cyprus at Christmas?" I asked.

"No. I mean, don't get me wrong, I love it in summer. It's paradise. But how I always long for one old-fashioned Christmas here ... back home, where I belong."

"You don't drink, do you, Mae?"

"No ... no ... I don't. It's not that I don't like a glass of sweet sherry or red wine but..."

"Are you sure you wouldn't like to go to the watchnight service across the road with Mrs Gillfillan tonight?" I asked. "After all, you'll be alone all evening here."

"No, not really. You know, I was married in December 1969. I often thought afterwards that it would have been nice to have had carols at the wedding service rather than the normal hymns that we chose." She looked pensive and then smiled. "I've always loved Christmas music, ever since I was a small child here at Muffberry Gruff Primary, when the music teacher taught us The First Noel in primary three.

Looking back on the wedding ceremony, it would have been more fitting if I'd chosen Abide With Me."

"But isn't that what they sing at funerals?" I asked.

"Yes, exactly."

"But you and your husband were the Liz Taylor and Richard Burton of Sandy Beach. The Posh and Becks of your day."

"Yes, on the surface it was a dream match," she said "But that was just the veneer." Her lips began to curl and her eyes penetrated the past painfully. "You see, my husband, once he started to gain success and national recognition for his football skills, changed completely."

"In what sense?"

"Well, he started to appear on TV. Interviewed on Match of the Day and other programmes. Then, suddenly, it all started to go to his head. Thought he was the new Georgie Best, so he did."

"And you fell into the shadows," I said.

"Yes, but it wasn't just that. I initially shared in it and enjoyed it all: the glittering parties and all that. But what soon became obvious and then unbearable was that he was a notorious womaniser, and I suppose always had been. I became the woman who had bourn his kids but little else. Others soon took priority over me." She shook her head. "Yes, many others."

"But you've moved on now, haven't you? You've established a new life for yourself, a place in the sun."

"Have I?" she asked. "I wouldn't say that."

"How come you went to live in Cyprus?" I asked.

"It's a long story. Are you prepared to listen?"

"Go on," I said.

"After my first husband divorced me, I met this good-time guy. Max was his name. The kids had left school and were finding their own way in life. Max enjoyed the nightlife: clubs, top-class restaurants, exotic foreign holidays. And he really liked me. He showered me with expensive gifts – jewellery, clothes, bouquets – until I thought I was the queen of the world. Then he asked me to marry him. When my first marriage was on the rocks, I threw myself into my work as a nurse. It was an escape. After all, it got me out of the house and away from the endless arguments and rows." She stopped and sighed. "Max said that he would look after me and I'd never have to work again. After our engagement, we set up a love nest in a lovely converted old farmhouse in the countryside. The wedding ceremony was organised, the reception booked, and guests invited. Then, a week before the wedding, he told me, in a voice as cold as ice, that he had gone off me and met someone else. The engagement was off and I had to vacate the house. He sold the place shortly after and went to live with his new girlfriend in Florida."

"I see. I'm sorry to hear that but what has this got to do with you moving to Cyprus?"

"I'm setting the scene for that. Want to hear more?"

"Go on," I said.

"I was on my own for a few years after that. The children took after their father in nature and personality. They took his side after the divorce and rarely visited. I decided it was time to be alone and that it was best that way. I was at least content with my own company. Then, one summer, I went on holiday to Cyprus for two weeks. I met this Greek guy, Stavros, who owned a bar in the resort where I stayed. He swept me off my feet with his passionate Mediterranean ways and so we embarked on a relationship. I moved to Cyprus to be with him but after a couple of years, and on my 55th birthday, he announced that he was trading me in for a much younger model, a young Danish woman who had visited his bar, like me, while she was on holiday on the island. And me? Well, I wasn't twenty-five. I wasn't even thirty-five. I just couldn't compete with her and so he, too, left me. I realised, if only too late, that I had gotten involved with yet another notorious womaniser."

"But you stayed on in Cyprus after the relationship ended."

"Yes. All my belongings were there and it meant a lot of hassle, never mind the expense of moving back here."

"So, that`s it then."

"I`m afraid it is. I certainly pick them when it comes to men," she said.

"I suppose you never know how people are going to turn out."

"No, but I`ve often ignored the warning signals," she said, shaking her head.

"And what about the children?" I inquired.

"Yes, what about the children indeed," she said. "I have three children but, you know, I often think I failed as a mother, failed miserably, looking back."

"In what way?"

"Well, they say now, as adults, that I was too busy working and wasn`t there for them. But they fail to understand why I worked such long hours and did so much overtime."

"Where are they now?"

"My eldest son lives in London with his wife. She doesn`t like me, so we never see each other but what I don`t understand is why, after so many years, he doesn`t make any effort to contact me, his mum. Then there`s my daughter. She works in New York; has done for ten years. I occasionally get a Christmas card from her. Then there`s my youngest son. He turned out to be a bit of a bad penny. I never see or hear from him at all. He`s been inside a few times for drug pushing, theft, and all the rest. I tried my best for them when they were young, I really did. I cared for and loved them so much, tried to bring them up to be decent. I … I..."

As tears welled up in her eyes, I tried to console her and make her see some positive light beyond the gloom.

"I`ve had an awful life," she confessed. "None of the men in my life treated me very well in the end. I was practically penniless when

Max put me out of the farmhouse. Threw me out on the streets more or less. That's why I never have a drink in public. If I have so much as a glass of wine, I start to cry. It seems to bring it all back to me. When Mrs Gillfillan asked me to the watchnight service, my instinct was to accept her invitation but if I go into church and hear the organ play the old, familiar carols and I join in the singing, I know that I would break down and cry like a baby. I would think of the happy days at Muffberry Gruff Primary or when my own kids were growing up, the special years, or when I attended Sunday school at Saint Aidans along with my older sisters all those years ago. Do you think I'm just a sentimental old fool?" She wiped her wet cheeks with her right palm and her tears stopped.

"No, not at all. I think you have good reason to cry and long for the past," I said.

"It's funny that we should meet, you remembering me from childhood. You know, come to think of it, I do vaguely remember you."

"It is funny, isn't it?"

"And what about you?"

"Me?"

"Yes, relationship-wise, where do you stand?"

"Don't talk to me about relationships. Yes, relationships, don't go there. I've had four major relationships in my life. In fact, I've been married twice but one day I woke up and found that I was on my own. It's not what I chose, just what life has awarded me. I also have two children, whom I seldom see. They went to live with their mother after the divorce. I haven't seen them for donkey's ages. Like you, I often ask myself where I've gone wrong."

Mae listened attentively and nodded patiently as if she had, perhaps, already guessed my story.

The boughs of holly that Mrs Gillfillan had cut from the bush in the garden heavily decked the elaborate mantelpiece, the top of the clock, and the window ledges, with bright red berries smiling in between the deep green of the prickly leaves.

By chance, fate had thrown Mae Laurence and myself together, once again and in very different circumstances from our last meeting. We sat there in the drawing room of the Aberlea Guest House, refugees from our own normal lives. We had returned to our spiritual home on this Christmas Eve, desperately trying to create a Christmas.

* * *

I dined with my aunt at 7 pm and kept company with her until about 10:30, during which time we watched what unfurled as the TV Christmas fare: popular films, carols, and ghost stories, many of which had been repeated year in and year out. The walk back to the B&B was quiet. A trickle of customers from pubs and the faithful, or at least those who liked to sing, making their way to Saint Ninians for Midnight Mass or the watchnight services at Saint Aidans or Saint Johns. The lights from Saint Aidans shone through the arched stained glass windows and out onto the main road as the clock chimed 11 pm. I wandered at a leisurely pace past the railings and the sombre facade of Muffberry Gruff Primary, which, half hidden by the darkness, declared itself present. I pulled my scarf around my neck. It was now bitterly cold and frost sparkled on the school walls and black railings. I stopped and looked towards the apple trees at the far end of the playground. Sure enough, as I had expected, the ten children appeared out of the darkness and started to move towards me. They giggled in the innocence of childhood freedom, and all greeted me in unison. I was, yet again, shocked that they were still playing outside, alone at what was now well past eleven. The children smiled wide, unashamed smiles and their eyes sparkled in innocent wonder as if silvery, distant stars. As they spoke, I felt a purity in their voices that shone from their very young beings.

They embarked, with great excitement, on a series of Christmas carols from See Amid the Winters Snow to Good King Wenceslas.

"And what is Santa Claus going to bring you tonight?" I asked.

"He brings us everything we have ever wanted," said the little lad with the Rupert badge.

The little red-haired boy continued. "But you see, we are always very happy, so in many ways, Saint Nicholas is eternally with us. He brings us presents every day."

A jolly voice from behind them said, " You see, sir, where we live now, well, it's Christmas every day."

"Where about do you live?" I asked curiously.

"We are from The Waverley," they all said together, though in various tones.

"It must be nice to be on holiday for a whole fortnight," I said. "Who is your teacher?" It had been at least forty years since I had last crossed the school's threshold and most probably I did not know any of the current teachers.

"Our teacher? Why it's Miss Sangster, of course."

"Miss Sangster? Miss Sangster?" I asked, somewhat aghast. "But, she was my teacher all those years ago. Why, she must be a hundred, if she's a day."

The children, all ten of them, turned silent and did not reply. They stared at me for a few silent seconds. The silence was then followed by the sweetest and most innocent of smiles.

"Well," I said. "It's really chilly. I must get back to the guest house and have a warm nightcap. Tomorrow's going to be a big day."

The eldest of the children spoke in reply. "Of course, for tomorrow is Christmas Day. Not just *any day* but Christmas Day."

I looked at him and recalled how magical Christmas had been to me as a child. "Indeed, it was my favourite day when I was a child," I said. "And I'm sure it must be yours too."

A small, skinny, blond-haired lad looked up and, smiling, said, "Oh, yes. You see, where we are now, it's Christmas every day. Every day is Christmas Day and full of festive cheer." Then all the children, in a wondrous, joyful voice, chanted together. *"For we are here to dispel all fear and come to spread the Christmas cheer."* They then proceeded to sing together, *"To spread the Christmas cheer,"* which they repeated over and over again. Finally, each one, individually, shouted out, "Happy Christmas!" They walked farther and farther away from me and then, suddenly, snowflakes began to fall, at first sparsely but then heavier and heavier still. Within a few minutes, the whole place was within a thick veil of snow as the children`s festive cries grew fainter until they seemed to disappear completely. They had gone. I could hear the muted sound of the pipe organ coming from the watchnight service across the road.

I opened the door of the guest house and entered its cosy refuge. There was no one about in the hall or drawing room. The old, holly-decked clock ticked on in a tranquil world that belonged only to Christmas Eve. A deep, silent stillness fell over the house and settled into the core of my heart.

* * *

Mrs Gillfillan had placed a small bottle of Buck's Fizz next to my cup at the breakfast table. It had snowed all night and was snowing still. It had indeed turned into a true white Christmas, just as old Bing had dreamt about in the song. Mae arrived at the breakfast room bleary-eyed, a good fifteen minutes after me, just as I had consumed the last of the sparkling Buck's Fizz.

"I slept so well last night. I can`t remember the last time I slept so well without a sleeping tablet. Awful things, so they are," she said.

"Oh, by the way, Mae," I said. "You know The Waverley?"

"Of course I know The Waverley," she said. "It was where I was born at the end of the war."

"You were born there?"

"Yes, that used to be the poorest area of town in those days but I tell you something: Its inhabitants had self-respect. They may not have had much but they taught their children politeness and were always well-dressed, even if it was in the best rags or hand-me-downs. They were honest and pure at heart and carried their poverty with dignity."

"Can I ask, who was your teacher at Muffberry Gruff?"

"Well, I had a few but the one who taught me for three years was Miss Sangster."

"And that was back in the 1950s?"

"That`s right. She was no spring chicken then. She`s been dead for at least twenty years. She died aged 99. I remember it well because there was a big article about it in The Herald and Advertiser."

"Yes, she was my teacher as well back in the 1960s. I know that she retired in 1969 but she was nearer 70 than 60 then. I always thought that The Waverley was demolished around the same time as she retired." "Oh, yes, it was. It was demolished in 1970 to make way for luxury flats. After that, they ceased to call that area The Waverley. They renamed it Stonefields Park."

"In 1970?"

"Yes but you see, part of the original Waverley, the collection of sprawling tenements built between Medieval times and the Victorian era, were deemed a health hazard. Then, of course, there was what happened in the early 1940s."

"What do you mean?"

"Well, the lower half of The Waverley received a direct hit from a German bomber and was flattened. It killed ten children. I remember all that because they all went to Muffberry Gruff School with my eldest sister. Some of them were in her class. It was a horrific tragedy for the town, even at a time when there was a bombing raid every night. My own family was left badly shaken by it all but thank god, they were unharmed. The worse thing about it was that it happened late on Christmas Eve."

Mrs Gillfillan entered the room carrying plates with our respective breakfasts. Mae looked at me inquisitively.

"You look like you`re in another world. What are you thinking about?"

"It's ... Well ... It's ... The last few nights, I spoke to children who told me that they lived in The Waverley."

Mrs Gillfillan stopped in her tracks just as she was about to exit the breakfast room. "Why, the children of Muffberry Gruff," she said in a most particular manner, as if she knew more about the issue than she cared to say. A certain aura came over her face. Then, in silence, she moved on.

The bells from the church across the road pealed jubilantly in celebration at the birth of the Christ Child.

"You know, I don't know what it is," said Mae, "but I feel ever so good, a lightness of heart, as if a burden has been lifted from me. I think I'll put on a bit of lippy, don my fake fur coat, and go to the Christmas service across the road. Oh! And I really wouldn't mind a Buck's Fizz when I come back."

The bells were now ringing triumphantly. Whether they were tuneful or not, I failed to notice, for it was Christmas Day, my favourite day when I was a child on Aragon Street and opened my presents from Santa long before dawn in the light of a warm hearth and the unique aroma of a fir tree.

I have stayed at the Aberlea Guest House on several occasions since and have passed the playground of Muffberry Gruff as often, yet I have never seen the mysterious children again, except perhaps on one occasion, late one Christmas Eve, when I swear I could hear, coming from behind the apple trees, the faintest sound of impish laughter in the cold of the frosty silent night.

We come to spread good cheer.

Chapter 2

HIGH HEDGE HOUSE

T he hours were long against a misty winter's afternoon. The black and white of bovine bodies could be seen faintly on the neighbouring fields that climbed the lower hills surrounding the small estate that High Hedge Grove looked out on. High Hedge House, home to the Fitzstevens family since the 13th century, was now much dilapidated and in need of repair. Remnants of the original Medieval building were still evident in the east wing. These included the gable, with its tiny windows and low door, built presumably to accommodate the short stature of our Medieval forefathers. The present incumbent was the Honourable Persephone Fitzstevens, named after a woman in Greek mythology, by parents who were obsessed with classical Greece and had spent several years of their early married life among the archaeologists and ancient sites of Hellenic civilization. Her twin brother had been given the name Ulysses and they had spent part of their childhood in different areas of what is now known as modern-day Greece. It was a heady dream of blue skies and bright sunshine as their parents indulged in their passion for the Hellenic ancients and Persephone and Ulysses danced an unending merry dance amid olive trees and tangled vines as they triumphantly proclaimed their childhood. It was all, however, cut abruptly short when Ulysses caught meningitis and died, all within the space of a summer's day. The music veered suddenly off-key and the carousel of bright, blue, sunny skies violently spiralled into the air. Life was never the same again. Persephone soon found herself disembarking from a ship at Southampton amid grey skies and torrential rain on a cold late November's day. Her memories were of misery that was written in the autumnal British sky and etched with grief on the faces of her parents.

Her first few weeks were spent at the home of a great aunt in London's Mayfair, just off Berkley Square. The home's dining room featured an unending long table, where she and her parents sat at one end and her great aunt sat at the opposite, the aunt a distant figure to be feared and respected but certainly not loved. The London days, so dominant in the initial dull, cold turmoil of her first month back in her parents' native land, soon evaporated into a long, boring train journey that had been initiated at King's Cross and seemed to take an age that, after it had left the metropolitan confines of London, sped past fields and villages, clad in thick white snow. They arrived at the tiny station of Westbrook, which consisted of a short platform and the cottage of a railway employee. A chauffeur in a shiny new black car awaited them. He loaded their luggage into the back of the vehicle and then drove cautiously through the narrow clearings along the country road.

After a drive of twenty minutes or so, they approached what seemed, to seven-year-old Persephone, to be a pair of giant gates gilded in bright white snow that Saint. Peter himself might have presided over. They opened onto a long tree-lined drive that advanced onto the concourse of the unusual facade of High Hedge House, which hung heavily with its heavy white endowment of freshly fallen snow. The entrance opened onto a large hall that prided itself on a tall fir tree shimmering in its glittering glory, with colourful baubles and the flickering lights of tiny candles that burned in dainty tin holders, for it was the afternoon of Christmas Eve. An old woman, who sported an elegant bun with a large black velvet bow, bent over to greet them in a frozen, controlled show of cordiality. However, Persephone noticed that her eyes glistened with the same warmth as the Christmas tree in all its festive splendour.

"This is your grandmother," said Persephone's father. The old woman looked lovingly down at the small figure that was her granddaughter. That evening, Persephone could feel a deep, warm winter's glow touch her heart and welcome her to her ancestral home. It was a warmth that transcended the cold snow of winter and one that she felt more at ease with than the bright Aegean sun. Christmas Eve had finally found her and welcomed her, in all its magical mystery, into the cosy fireside of its bosom, in this, her true home. Ulysses, her brother, whom she dearly missed so much, somehow seemed to slip into a niche of the past, yet still sat next to Persephone in spirit, as if encouraging her to enjoy the moment and continue without him, secure and strong in her new home, where she was to discover hidden gardens, mysterious mazes, and secret rooms, meet new friends, and, when none were at hand, invent them.

The years of happiness grew in abundance around her.

* * *

Persephone had celebrated her 73rd birthday on November 10th and awaited the arrival of her only grandson, Jamie, one month later on the afternoon of December 10th. She often thought back, especially in December, of her first days at High Hedge House, in the earlier part of the century, when her cares were light and Christmas glowed with a special holy light that was difficult to describe in human terms. Jamie Montague-Lovat jumped spiritedly out of a grey Bentley that had seen a bit of wear and tear but that Persephone was much attached to. As it provided a reasonably comfortable ride from A to B, she saw little sense in going to the extravagance of buying a new one. The strong winter's sun blinded Alf, the chauffeur, as he drove up to the main entrance. He made to open the door for master Jamie, who did not wait on Alf but turned the handle himself, as if all his patience had run out, to embark on this new adventure. Persephone ran down the stone steps of the entrance and hugged him with a spontaneity that she had inherited from her Greek upbringing in a land where emotion was never suppressed and expressions of affection were never hidden behind a collective, controlled British reserve. Her arthritis came and went with good days and bad days but in general, it was a pain that gnawed rather than ached and one she still, at least most of the time, found bearable. Jamie hadn't felt so excited since the Halloween party the preceding autumn, which he had enjoyed more thoroughly, than the annual Guy Fawkes Night firework display and bonfire that his neighbours hosted each November 5th. This year, the event had proved to be a disappointing, damp washout. His mother, who had never been particularly religious, had converted to Catholicism upon her marriage to Jamie's stepfather, an American, whose Lancashire ancestors, during penal times, had hidden priests in secret passages. She had, in fact, to everyone's surprise, taken it all extremely seriously, and had grumbled that she saw no reason to celebrate burning Catholics and no longer approved of bonfires on November 5th. Jamie had, in all honesty, never been that fond of Guy Fawkes Night and had enjoyed it primarily because it was a landmark on the journey to Christmas. Jamie's father remained in Chad, where he continued in his role as an ambassador. His mother and stepfather had gone to spend Christmas with the stepfather's family in New England. Jamie, who did not care much for his stepfather's relatives, had vehemently protested at having to spend Christmas with them in the States. His mother, driven to distraction by his stubborn opposition to the festive plans, had sent him off to High Hedge House, relieved to end his unending tantrums on the subject. He had spent part of his summer holidays at High Hedge House some years back, when he was ten, but he had never visited High Hedge at Christmas. Persephone was of the opinion that her daughter-in-law was far too interested in being accepted by her husband's family, which she pursued regardless of Jamie's needs. While appreciating that Jamie was far from neglected or unloved, she believed that his mother had bypassed Jamie's best interests. Persephone had, since the herald of his visit, decided to ensure that his first Christmas at High Hedge House would be, above all, a pleasurable one that someday, when older, he might recall with fondness. Persephone was, however, at a loss as to how to entertain a 12-year-old child, and a boy at that. She knew that the current generation of 12-year-olds did not have the same interests as those of her generation. She did not keep up with current trends and did not know the latest craze in games or the hits by any contemporary pop singers. Persephone, in fact, had a terrible ignorance when it came to the charts and also bemoaned the fact that the last children's TV programme she had watched in its entirety had been an episode of Blue

Peter, which to her seemed only a couple of years before but had, in fact, been televised in early 1960.

When he entered the great hall, Jamie's eyes widened as he gasped at the place. His father had written and vividly described the annual grandiose Christmas tree and the lighted candles that the hall hosted, how they flickered behind the coloured baubles – something that, in the modern Christmas of mass-produced fairy lights, was completely new and fascinating to Jamie. Once he had investigated the tree, he firmly knew that this Christmas would be somewhat different from what he was used to and one he would most definitely enjoy.

Jamie slept a deep and sound sleep under the fat, feather-filled duvet of the four-poster oak bed, with its intricate carvings of the apostles – Matthew, Mark, Luke, and John – on each of its dark wooden posts. He awoke in the morning to the congenial winter sun's rays as they peaked in through the windows, draped in heavy crimson brocade curtains. After he had washed and dressed himself, he made his way down the majestic stairway, created during an age of opulence, towards the small breakfast room. An ageing woman with a white linen cap covering her grey curly hair poked her head through the corner of the door.

"I've made them scrambled but if you prefer them fried, I'll do them fried tomorrow. I've made the toast well done, as Mistress Persephone likes it, and I've put a good portion of bacon on this here plate. Lovely bacon so it is, lovely bacon, beautiful. The best, I tell you. I had a bit on a hot roll at six this morning myself and I can tell, it's lovely, lovely so it is. Now there's tea in the pot here and some freshly brewed coffee over there. If you need anything else, just give me a shout."

"Yes, thanks I will," said Jamie. His eyes wandered onto a plate of edibles dotted with currents that were piled one on top of the other in a pyramid arrangement. "And what are those?"

"Oh, those are your bagels, aren't they? And I tell you, they are the most beautiful bagels you have ever tasted. Lovely so they are, lovely, absolutely beautiful. I had a couple with fresh butter at six this morning and I can say they are beautiful but lovely." With that, she left the room and Jamie found himself alone to consume his breakfast.

His deep sleep had made him hungry. The breakfast room had a bright and airy feel about it. The walls were plain bar a simple watercolour painting in a wooden frame: an image of the Acropolis that had been painted by Persephone`s father.

After breakfast, Jamie felt rather full. He had consumed all of the bacon and five of the bagels, which he had coated with thick layers of marmalade. He walked across the entrance hall to the drawing room, where Persephone was sipping a cup of warm coffee.

"I never eat much for breakfast during the week. I usually just have a couple of cups of coffee and a slice of toast. Of course, I always eat a large breakfast at weekends, something a bit special, a bit *other* from the rest of the week, as it were."

Jamie looked up to her in a particular way. "I see," he said without altering his expression.

"Have you slept well?" enquired his grandmother.

"Indeed, I have. In fact, I have slept very well."

"And have you eaten well?"

"Yes, indeed I have. I have eaten so much that if you were to offer me chocolate, I would have to politely refuse," he answered, patting his stomach.

"And what would you like to do today?" asked Persephone, broadening her smile.

"I should like to wander around this huge house and explore the grounds. The last time I came here, I was unwell and confined to bed for most of my stay. Then, when mother came, she forbade me from exploring the place, saying that I wasn`t strong enough and would only tire myself out and that if I got lost in the grounds, she did not have the energy to come looking for me."

"Then explore the old building and grounds, you shall. It's all part of your Fitzstevens heritage," said Persephone.

"Who was that old woman?" asked Jamie nonchalantly.

"Which lady?"

"The old woman at breakfast. Who is she?"

"Why, that's Dolly Perry. She's the housekeeper's cook."

"Does she live here too?"

"Not exactly, no. She lives in Leafy Cottage."

"Where's that?" quizzed Jamie as he cocked his head in curiosity

"It sits amidst the trees at the back of the house, just before you cross the stream at the old stable bridge."

Jamie's curiosity was not yet satisfied. "Is she Alf's wife?"

"Oh, no, no, Alf's wife left him many a long year ago."

"Does he live here?"

"He lives in a basement flat at the east gable, directly next to the garage."

Jamie suddenly seemed to lose interest in the who's who of High Hedge House and wandered over to the tall bay window, which was home to a gigantic, dangling wandering sailor plant. The plant had, according to Persephone, died at various times over the years but had been reborn again and again. Its leaves, now flourished, had been resurrected from the dead like Eurydice, beloved of Orpheus in Greek mythology. Persephone had delighted in the opera during her first years at High Hedge Grove estate and had oft, on weekends, been rushed off to London to attend the well-known classics of Covent Garden, of which Gluck's Orpheus and Eurydice was her favourite. It had reminded her of her Greek childhood, which lived on in heady, cloudy memories of days gone by.

* * *

The dark grey days of December moved on, occasionally tinted in sparkling white frost that turned into delicate, fluffy, white snow. High Hedge House appeared amid the fields as some optical illusion in a white coat of fur.

In the days that proceeded the 20th of December, Jamie became the recipient of a large, brown-papered package that was, indeed, tied up with strings. It was a parcel from his mother that contained his Christmas present.

DO NOT OPEN UNTIL DEC.25TH, it stated in large, black letters of stark honesty, inscribed by a domineering, thick felt pen. For some inexplicable reason, he felt no great urge to open it. He had, in the weeks of December, become embroiled in everything High Hedge House: its attractions and its sheer mystery, which day by day continued to enthral him more and more. The hedges, cut into the form of giant peacocks, cast huge shadows over the driveway as the sun set at dusk and were given rebirth as hideous monsters visible in the deep black of a winter's night.

One afternoon, while he was walking with Alf through the grounds, Jamie's eyes came across a certain tree which stirred a curiosity in him.

"What a strange-looking tree," said Jamie, raising his voice, aghast at its perpendicular appearance studded with thick, lumpy bark that, to Jamie, had a somewhat otherworldliness to it, something that, to him, would look quite at home in his favourite TV programme, Dr. Who, which featured Patrick Troughton as the ageless Doctor and Frazer Heinz as Jamie, whom Jamie Montague-Lovat had a special attachment to due to them sharing the same name. Some days, he would rush around the dark corridors and spiral staircases of High Hedge House, pretending to be Jamie from Dr. Who, in the middle of one of his greatest adventures.

"That tree's a funny one right enough," said Alf. "Its story is as ugly as itself."

"What do you mean?" asked Jamie.

"A man was hanged on it back in 1690."

"Was he really, Alf?" asked Jamie in disbelief.

"Yes, he was, really," laughed Alf. "But don't you be going having any sympathy with him. No, no, he was a thief and a notorious murderer."

"A thief and murderer?"

"Yes, that's right. He deserved his sentence, so he did."

"And he was killed just like that."

"Yes he was, as you say, just like that, but it was in 1690 ... a bit before my time."   "I see. So what is your time? I mean, when were you born?"

"Me? Why, I was born at Micklemas,1902, I was."

"That's a long time ago."

"I suppose it seems that to you but it's flown by in no time."

"You're nearly as old as Dr. Who."

"And how old's he?"

"He's very, very old."

"You see all the white snow that covers the fields and trees?"

"Yes."

"Well, in the summer months, they are all bright green and the borders of the lawns are covered in an abundance of colourful flowers."

"Oh, yes. I remember from the last time I was here but you were away, away on holiday."

"Yes, indeed, I was, gone to Bournemouth, so I was."

"Oh, yes, Bournemouth. My mother took me there once and we went to the beach."

"Look at the time! We really need to go back to the house. Dolly will have prepared afternoon tea and your grandmother will be waiting in the lesser drawing room for you to enjoy it together."

The heat of the drawing room was most welcome after the freezing cold of the grounds. Dolly had made toast with melted cheese, and cake stands were stacked heavily with homemade sponges and scones. The tea was Earl Gray with its own distinct aroma. Persephone poured it from a rose-patterned teapot.

"Have you had a nice day?" she enquired as the spout hit the delicate top of the china cup.

"Yes, every day is nice here. Sometimes it would be nice to have someone to play with. Don't any of the children come up from the village?"

"No, not really. There's a shortage of children, so to speak. The last generation of women was either childless or had only one child. It really was a most peculiar situation. The very few children who were here moved to the big cities with their parents, who went there to find work. The ones who are left I hardly know and have hardly even set eyes on."

"So there are no children I could play with, then."

"Well the ones I can think of, and there aren`t many, are either far too old or years too young for you to keep company with. You`ll have to make do with your own company."

"My own company?" asked Jamie, raising the tone of his voice in an exaggerated question mark.

"Yes, your own company," repeated Persephone. "Don`t malign it, your own company. Childhood can be an imaginative and most creative affair."

"What do you mean?" asked Jamie.

"Well, for example, I was often left to play on my own when I first arrived at High Hedge Grove in those far-off heady days. I amused myself by pretending that different parts of the estate and even the house itself were far-off countries that I gave names to. There were also all my wonderful little friends whom I had created in my imagination and whose portraits I had drawn with crayons. I gave them all their own little histories and their own little traits, good and bad. I even insisted on having a place set for them nightly at dinner and always sent notes on their behalf to Father Christmas. Grandma would often step in as some imaginary adult intermediary," she said. "I`m not sure if she was always so willing to play those roles, but she usually did, most likely out of some sense of love." Persephone stood and viewed the garden from the window. "Yes, a good old sport was dear Grandma." She sighed sentimentally. Then screwed up her eyes as if to view something that appeared minuscule from her vantage point.

"Can I watch TV now? Children`s hour should be starting soon. There`s a good story on Jackanory by that well-known comedian. What`s his name again?"

Persephone looked blank. "I wouldn`t know," she said. "Go on into the supper room and Dolly will switch it on. Are you sure you have had enough to eat?"

"Yes," he replied. "Enough until supper time."

Persephone made her way upstairs to an ante-room, off her bedroom, where she kept items of little value but which held a special position in her heart. She rummaged in drawers and bookshelves, piled high with papers and reading material of sorts, until the sun had set and darkness had settled completely over the house. Artificial light became a necessity. A large cardboard file tied with a large red bow emerged from under a dictionary on the very top of the bookshelf

"Ah! Here it is," she gasped in a positive breath.

At 8 o`clock exactly, Dolly hit the large brass gong

in the entrance hall, which proclaimed the immediate serving of supper. Jamie had already scoffed down all of his hors d'oeuvres by the time Persephone arrived in the dining room, spruced up, if not altogether dressed up, for the main meal of the day. Old age had dulled her once enthusiastic appetite and she now ate comparatively little: a few fried courgettes, maybe a sautéed potato or two. Puddings were inclined to be light and were often replaced by fruit: a fresh pineapple or even a Macedonian fruit salad. Cheese was a definite no, as, again with age, it seemed to deprive her of sleep if consumed in the evenings. Jamie had finished his crème caramel and was sitting contentedly in his chair, hands upon his lap, while Persephone sipped on a small glass of Mavrodaphne dessert wine from Patras. She left the glass empty, apart from a small drop of the sweet, deep red substance, then put it to one side. She picked up and handed, to Jamie, the dilapidated cardboard file tied with a faded, red bow, which she had found earlier on top of the bookcase. "I thought you could have these. You might as well take them now."

"What, you mean this is some sort of present?"

"I suppose in a roundabout way it is," replied Persephone.

Jamie undid the bow with pangs of curiosity in his fingers. He took the folder apart and then excitedly pulled out a thick batch of drawings, created and coloured with crayons.

"What`s this?" he cried out. "Did you draw these?"

Persephone looked affectionately at the crude efforts at drawing and the faded, torn edges of the papers, which now looked so very dated and held some unseen trademark that was most definitely that of another era.

"Yes, I drew them all," said Persephone with an emerging grin on the side of her mouth. "All of them. I did indeed draw, a long time ago."

Jamie inspected the drawings of children`s faces and childlike depictions of houses and flowers. They seemed to spring out of the coarse grey paper and greet him in a roundabout, peculiar sort of way.

"These," said Persephone "are the drawings of my childhood friends, here at High Hedge House. That`s to say, my dear, dear imaginary friends."

"The ones you told me about?" asked Jamie.

"Yes, the very same ones."

He went through the pictures one by one.

"Who`s he?"

"Why, that`s Gilbert."

"And this one?"

"That`s his sister Totty."

"And him?"

"That`s their youngest brother Benjamin."

"And this one here, who is he?"

"That`s the other brother Robin."

"And is this their little sister?"

"No, she`s their cousin Hildegard."

"And her?"

"That`s Hildegard`s sister Maizie and the one you are about to look at is Marmaduke, her baby brother."

" I think that's a strange name. It's like someone's title added to a breakfast."

"Yes, it does, doesn't it? I believe I had a distant cousin who bore the same name." Persephone exuded a subdued laugh. "It's funny. I hadn't thought of my little friends for years until I mentioned them to you."

As Jamie looked at them over and over again, the grandfather clock ticked on in its time with the hypnotic tick-talk that gave the place a soothing, calm air, as if declaring that, no matter what might happen, everything was most assuredly alright.

High Hedge House sang its very own Christmas carol which its December environs had composed. It flowed out melodiously in its jolly, lullaby-ish notes and Jamie soon found them on his lips and teasing at his vocal cords. Soon, he, too, began to hum the unique, mysterious carol. His nails delicately pressed into the dotted outline of the area of the advent calendar with "22" inscribed boldly upon it. Then he opened it to reveal a pleasant cherubic face "Only three doors left," he said to himself as he browsed at numbers 23, 24, and 25, eager to open them. It was a more up-to-date British calendar that culminated in the final, great door opening on December 25th as opposed to the older, more traditional, German-style advent calendars that climaxed in an extraordinary illustration opened on December 24th, when Christmas and present giving were celebrated in German states. The sky gave off little sunlight and remained imprisoned in dull, greyish shades that did not give any promise of colour or brightness, instead staying true and loyal to its very own winter self in its own extraordinary tentacles of integrity.

After breakfast, Persephone had been chauffeured by Alf to the train station, where she had boarded the 10 o'clock train to London. There, she said, she had some business with her solicitor, who was based on Kensington High Street. Persephone found the London of the swinging 60s somewhat perplexing and yet, at the same time, a refreshing period of renewal that released the sentiments of her classical Greek childhood. It was so contradictory and far removed from the

British stiff upper lip and stubborn Victorian stuffiness that had persisted well into the 20th century, suffocating her Bohemian upbringing and stifling the free spirit she had inherited from such unconventional parents. Persephone had, only too late, begun to understand and appreciate the sentiments of the swinging London of the so-revolutionary 1960s which were now coming to an end. Somewhat bemused by their values, Persephone now realised what it was all about. Now, only as a latecomer, had it dawned on her that not only were *the times a-changing* but they had, in fact, already changed, been drowned by an over-optimism that would forever immortalise it as a *Golden Era.* Christmas, on the other hand, clung to its Victorian past – a part of Victorianism that Persephone was still most fond of. During her early years at High Hedge, her dear, late grandmother had often moaned that things had never been the same since the death of old Queen Victoria. The monarch who had been much loved by her people and who some thought to be immortal had died in the arms of her favourite grandson, Kaiser Wilhelm of Germany. Her passing had seen a horrendous war with her favourite grandson, followed by another with the land of his birth, where her much loved and mourned Prince Albert had breathed his first breath. Persephone`s father had reluctantly fought in the Great War, in which he had been wounded, but he had survived and was spared from active combat in World War II. All of this and more had helped create her identity and made her the Honourable Persephone Fitzstevens, whom she rightly was.

Jamie had wandered restlessly around High Hedge Grove Estate, unsure of exactly what to do. He had looked at Persephone`s drawings of her imaginary friends over and over again since being presented with them. He had put them carefully back into their file and stored them in the bottom of the wardrobe, next to his bed. Before lunch, he had wandered farther than he had ever done on the grounds of High Hedge House, far beyond the stream, next to the old stable and into the Italian gardens with their carved hedges that took on the form of peacocks. Old, thatched cottages, with small, quaint diamond windows, had been deserted for years. He entered an enclosed lawn surrounded by fir trees that bowed heavily with white snow. There, he viewed a group of elderly pensioners playing croquet on the snow-covered lawn. At first, Jamie found nothing unusual about the scene. He stood at the edge of the lawn and observed them passively. The elderly players seemed oblivious to Jamie`s presence and continued to play on despite the depth of the snow, which only then occurred to him to be an extraordinary situation. The ladies wore small hats that exhibited pure white hair underneath the brims. The men wore distinguished caps and had large silver moustaches above their pale, aged lips. They continued with their game uninterrupted by young Jamie`s stares. They seemed at peace with themselves and manifested no need to converse with each other, as if a deep familiarity needed no trivial parlance. They were content in their firmly established company to comprehend each other without the shallow aid of words, and they made no issue of – and demanded nothing from – Jamie`s company. He inferred no nastiness from their non-observance of his presence. Upon leaving them, he made his way slowly back to High Hedge House for tea.

Jamie sat in the drawing room, waiting on the arrival of his grandmother. The premature night was falling. It was not quite the land of the midnight sun but certainly the land of dark afternoons. Dolly huffed and fussed with a can of Brasso in one hand and a cloth in another as Jamie picked up a large framed black and white photo. Dolly noticed and came up behind him.

"Beautiful it was. Look at that veil. A true masterpiece of Flanders lace. Beautiful it was, and look at Miss Persephone and her betrothed on their wedding day. A beauty to behold. Her looking so beautiful, and him, her groom, so handsome, so tall. I remember it well so I do, even if I was but a slip of a girl. Beautiful so it was, and her own parents dressed in Greek traditional costume. I found that a bit funny myself, if you ask me, so I say, but Miss Persephone looked beautiful in that veil with its delicate little roses and her white satin dress. Pity that what happened to it happened.

"What do you mean what happened to it happened?" asked Jamie.

"Well, as I say, what happened to it happened. You see, my previous incumbent, Mary Mathews, a cousin of my mother's, a silly sort of character, decided to give the dress a thorough wash to take out the stains incurred on the wedding day and the dirt engrained by the years. She washed it most carefully by hand one November's afternoon, when the rain poured torrentially, and thought it a good idea to dry it indoors, in front of the great fireplace in the kitchen, which gave off a great heat. But you see, the fire gave off such a heat that the delicate wedding dress went up in flames."

"Went up in flames?"

"Yes, just like a small bonfire on Guy Fawkes Night."

"Was it completely destroyed?"

"Mary Mathews piled buckets and basins of water over it but it was all in vain. Burned to a cinder it was."

"Oh, dear!"

"She was lucky the whole house didn't go up, foolish woman, but a beautiful dress it was."

Persephone eventually made her entrance through the door of the drawing room. Dolly immediately stopped polishing, lay the can of Brasso on top of a crocheted doily, which her own hands had produced, and poured the tea from a silver pot into the wide-mouthed cup that sat directly in front of Persephone, who then began to nibble at a smoked salmon sandwich laid out on a china tray.

She looked over at Jamie. "Do anything exciting today?"

"Every day and everything is exciting here," he said.

Indeed, everything about High Hedge House and its surrounding estate was redeeming and of deep fascination: the pseudo-Medieval gargoyles that glared down onto the smiling face of the wide lawn, the mysterious classical statues that peered at him through dense layers of ivy and foliage, the sudden narrow paths that led into circular clearings in the minuscule forest, furnished with marble toadstools and fairies. Tiny timber houses that may have once been inhabited by Snow

White stood almost hidden by the long grass that had been left to grow in the outlying parts of the grounds, which had an unkempt, rambling ambiance to them. No, one was certainly never bored at High Hedge House.

"I walked farther than I have ever done today," Jamie continued.

"Really," said Persephone. "Mind that you don't get too cold, wandering in the frost for hours on end." Memories came back to her of her brother Ulysses, and an overwhelming sense of protectiveness or even over-protectiveness came over her. "I wouldn't want you coming down with a bad cold or, God forbid, pneumonia. Not with Christmas on our doorstep."

High Hedge House was far more fun than his summer holidays in Spain, which he had found somewhat uninteresting – too much sand, and newly built concrete hotels could be boring after a week. There had been more than enough sand, sun, and sea, which, at the end of the three-week break, had become nothing but monotonous and predictable. Jamie had much enjoyed his September trip the year before to the Ivory Coast, where his father had been a diplomat. The two had passed a memorable holiday at the ocean there.

Persephone cut into a Victoria sponge, which was the ultimate in Dolly's baking skills. Its thick, fresh cream and jam oozed out onto her fork.

"Who are the old folk?" asked Jamie.

"What do you mean by *old folk*?"

"The old folk I saw playing a game in the snow. You know, what's it called? Not golf ... er ... croquet, yes, that's it."

" I can't think who you mean. Old folk? Unless it was maybe two of Dolly's elderly aunts but they're too old to be playing outside in this weather and Dolly hasn't mentioned anything about her having guests. I've no idea who they would be."

"Oh! There were more than two and they were not just women but some men as well."

"Well, I've no idea. On this estate?" Persephone looked through the window at the darkness. "The days will be longer after New Year's

Day. I like the summer days but I`m not sure if I like daylight in the late afternoon when it's still winter. It reminds me that my favourite time of year has passed and it`s time to strip the house of all decorations, of all that is special and extraordinary, and return to the mundane."

Persephone stood from her chair and made her way over to a sideboard, where she picked up a rather tatty, dog-eared hardback novel. Then she returned to sit in her chair and, with a contended, carefree sigh, opened its first page: A Christmas Carol by Charles Dickens. She flicked onto the second page and began to read.

* * *

Jamie slowly emerged from an undisturbed and deep sleep, enjoying the hazy, drifting feeling as he realised that it was finally, at last, Christmas Eve. So long had he looked forward to this special day and all its particular expectations. The huge fir tree had been delivered very early in the morning while he was still in slumbers beneath the sheets. Persephone thought it a good idea if Jamie participated in the great decorating process, along with herself, Dolly, and Alf. *"I heard the bells on Christmas Day, their old familiar carols sing,"* said Dolly in an effort to infuse more life in Jamie on this Christmas Eve. However, there was no need, for excitement and happiness in its extreme guise were slowly simmering inside him. Cardboard grocery boxes and bashed old hat boxes bursting with strands of tinsel and multi-coloured papered festoons were brought in procession into the great hall by a handful of part-time staff, engaged only at certain times of the year. All of them were now impaired by the years, yet still industrious and energetic. Steps were set up at both sides of the naked fir tree as the decorations were distributed among the gathering, who embarked on their seasonal mission. Dolly blew dust off the wings of a cherub while Alf attached red baubles to thick green branches that begged to be decorated. In no time at all, the tree took on a personality of its own as it donned its ultimate for the Nativity Feast: a royal personage dressed for a regal occasion by their valets.

"I really think Jamie should have the honour of doing this," said Persephone when all decorations were at last hanging on the tree. She held up an unusual star made from a large starfish that had been painted and covered in glue and glitter throughout the years. It had been brought from Greece by Persephone all those years ago and used ever since then for the crowning moment of the Christmas tree.

Just as Jamie placed the star on the pinnacle of the tree, the telephone could be heard ringing in its aggressively sharp tone, cutting into the serenity of the ceremony. Dolly ran off to pick up the clumsy black receiver. Then she ran back into the hall.

"Miss Persephone, it's a call from the USA, if you please."

Persephone looked at Jamie as she rushed to take the call "Oh, it must be your mother." She took the phone with a look of urgency as if President Johnson himself were about to give a briefing on some pending world issue. After a few brief minutes of questions and answers concerning Jamie, Persephone handed the receiver to him. His mother was concerned about his happiness in spending Christmas far away from her. But the truth be told, Jamie was having a far better time than he would have had he had gone to the States and, he didn`t mind spending Christmas far away from his mother, or his father, for that matter. After all, he did see his mother at least every day of the year. Exploring the mysterious nooks and crannies of the High Hedge Grove estate was a far more interesting prospect than any itinerary his parents might have dreamed up. The phone ended with his mother making kissing sounds on the American side. Jamie didn`t care for that much at all but exchanged a cordial "Happy Christmas" before putting down the receiver, which was then routinely dusted and polished by Dolly.

She then turned to Alf. "I`ve made you a big plate of ham sandwiches and a hot Ovaltine in the kitchen."

"You`re a good one," he said, smiling as he made his leave of the hall and went downstairs.

Jamie observed the glittering omnipotence of the newly decorated tree and felt a soft kick of contentment in his heart, coupled with a degree of pride in the team's achievement. That evening, after supper, he hung one of his longest socks next to the large fireplace in the hall and wrote a letter to Santa Claus, which he then threw, with much vigour, up the chimney. Finally, he retired to his bedroom with a dog-eared edition of a 1930s children's annual that he had found amid the soaring heights of one of the numerous bookcases lining so many of the rooms and halls. He had used portable steps to access it. As he drifted off to sleep, his thoughts turned to the group of elderly people he had seen on the grounds and how no one seemed to know exactly who they were.

* * *

The grandfather clock struck 11 pm. Its sharp chimes were audible throughout most of the house. Everyone had retired to bed at a civilized time. Jamie awoke, expecting it to be Christmas Day. Disappointed, he abruptly sat up in bed, then restlessly rose and looked out of the window onto the white grounds outside. Everything was still. The chimes had also awoken Persephone in her chamber, far along the corridor. She always had been a light sleeper on Christmas Eve, when her mind became a refuge for memories and sentiments of years past and mirrors of the house as it was in her childhood years. Jamie looked at the shadow that the moon created on the even, soft snow. Still was the night and the moon its master in the blip of time that was a piece in the great jigsaw of creation that portraits portrayed and inhabited as best mortals could but it was only eleven o'clock and Emmanuel was not quite with them. Persephone would rise early, though most likely later than Jamie, and go to the small church in the village for the matins of Christmas Day. She would take Jamie with her. She thought he would enjoy listening to and singing the carols. *"I heard the bells on Christmas Day their old familiar carols sing,"* she heard herself unconsciously utter. Her grandmother had taught her the much-loved poem, though most of it had dissolved into a forgotten blur.

Jamie, unaware of Persephone's sleepless state, stared at the mystical landscapes in the hope that Saint Nick might be lurking somewhere there. He had become curious as to the mystery of the seasonal character. Persephone also thought of Jamie and Saint Nick and how the jovial bearded grandfather, a Greek from Asia Minor, would soon end his sojourn as Christmas benefactor. When that happened, Christmas, to Jamie, as it had been to Persephone, would never be the same again. At this, she felt a pang of true sadness in her breast.

As Jamie sat admiring the beauty and the seasonal comfort of the snow, a group of winter-clad personages began to appear one by one in the view from the window. He had seen them before. Yes, they were the group of elderly people he had encountered playing croquet, whom no one seemed to know anything about, and they were making their way towards the house. The grandfather clock in the hall chimed midnight

"The Christ child is born," said Persephone to herself and the last stroke resounded throughout the great house.

* * *

They sat comfortably, feeling quite at home in the drawing room as if they had once had a familiar relationship with the place. They, the winter-clad personages whom Jamie had seen traversing the deep snow of the grounds outside, were now seated on the armchairs and sofas of the drawing room, their furs and tweeds discarded and hanging on coat stands in the hallway. Jamie heard the muffled chit-chat from his room. Out of great festive curiosity, he made his way downstairs to investigate. Was it perhaps a conversation between Santa Claus and his helpers? This would, of course, prove that the annual reincarnation of that most benevolent of saints *did*, in fact, occur. The assembled greeted Jamie with wide, infectious smiles and a full round of hearty Christmas wishes that were fit for the best of Christmas Days.

One of the elderly gentlemen stood up from his chair. "I don`t believe we have met on any of our previous visits," he said. "Permit me to introduce myself. My name is Gilbert and this is my sister Totty."

Smiling eyes came from the old girl through the thick lenses of rounded spectacles. She opened her clasped hands and turned her palms upwards. "And this is our brother Benjamin," she said.

"I`m pleased to meet you," said a bald man wearing a tweed waistcoat. "And may I ask, who you are?" he enquired cordially.

"I`m James ... Jamie ... Montague-Lovat. My grandmother is Persephone. I`m spending the Christmas holidays with her here at High Hedge House."

The assembled seniors all smiled as a unit and exuded a high and positive "Oh!" They then turned to one another.

"He`s her grandson."

"Fancy, this young chap`s her grandson."

"There is a family resemblance, I`d say."

"Oh, yes, most definitely."

They all chuckled amidst their comments.

"Oh, and I`m Robin, the other brother."

"Yes, we always call him *the other brother*," said Gilbert.

"A form of endearment, really," said Totty.

"Indeed," said Robin.

A woman in a dark green velvet bonnet with a feather decorating its left-hand side offered a hand to Jamie. "And I am Hildegard, their cousin, but lots of people assume I am their sister."

Totty nodded and piped up. "Yes, they do. We`ve always been very close, you know."

The old woman sitting next to her introduced herself. "And I`m the other cousin, Maizie."

A rather slim man who seemed to be a lot younger than the others, though still elderly and grey, stood and nodded his head amiably. "And I'm Marmaduke, the youngest of them all. I'm the brother of Maizie and Hildegard, cousin to the others."

"Oh, yes, I remember the name. Marmaduke, yes," said Jamie in an audible whisper. "How nice to meet you all but may I ask, who exactly are you? I mean, are you who I think you are? Is that possible?"

"Why, dear Jamie, we are all very good friends of your dear grandma," said Hildegard in a jolly tone.

"Yes. Indeed, we are all very good friends of dear Persephone," said Totty.

"Yes," said Gilbert. "In fact, we are as close as family to her, just as much as if she were another sister."

"Such a good friend to us is Persephone," said Maizie.

"Friends, you say. And what is your surname?" Jamie asked.

"Oh!" said Gilbert. Everyone laughed at the same time.

Totty cleared her throat. "Surname? Why, we haven't got one," she said.

Robin gave out a heartfelt belly full of laughs. "No, we haven't one."

"Because, I suppose, nobody ever thought to give us one," said Marmaduke earnestly.

"I see. Because no one thought to give you one," said Jamie. "But may I ask, and I don't want to be rude ... Are you my grandmother's imaginary friends?"

Robin looked at Jamie. "Yes, that's who we are. That's exactly who we are."

Jamie stood aghast, mouth wide open, and then he immediately sat, for assurance, down onto a stool as if the answer had exhausted him. "But you are imaginary. You are not supposed to really exist. That's the whole point of being imaginary."

"Yes, a figment of Persephone's imagination, a product of her childhood creativity, but we most definitely do exist," said Marmaduke. "Look at me. Am I not real?"

"But why ... How ... How on earth is it possible?" asked Jamie.

Totty smiled comfortingly. "You see, Jamie, we exist for the simple reason that Persephone's vivid imagination created us and brought us to life," she said.

"And now," said Benjamin, who had been the quietest of the group up till now. "*We are*, so, therefore, we exist."

Just then, a voice came through the open door of the drawing room. "It's been such a long time, such a long, long time." It was Persephone.

The seated group of seniors arose from their chairs as Persephone walked towards them all and exchanged hugs and kisses as warm as the hearth itself had been only some hours before.

"All of us together again, just like it used to be," said Hildegard.

"All the games on the lawn. All the larks we used to have," said Benjamin.

"Oh, yes, playing pirates. On the pond," said Maizie.

"Such happy times." Gilbert smiled. "And every Christmas you gave us tiny little gifts, all tied up in red ribbons."

"They were indeed very special times," said Totty.

"Indeed, they were." added Benjamin.

"And you've all come to see me again and at Christmas as well," said an overwhelmed Persephone.

"A true Christmas surprise!" said Robin.

"When was the last time you visited me?" asked Persephone.

Gilbert put his hand to his head. "Oh, let's see now, when would that have been, Totty?"

"I really can't remember the year but it was the Christmas Eve when you were in your 12th year."

"That's right, it would have been," said Persephone.

"All those years ago," said Marmaduke.

"And in that time we've all grown up and grown old," said Maizie as Persephone grabbed her hand.

"But, I still recognised you all," she said.

Jamie sat on the sofa and listened to them all.

"But you never visited me again after I was about 13. Why? Why was that?"

"Well, Persephone, you stopped thinking of us. You stopped playing games with us and then you stopped imagining things for us to do. We went out of your mind totally. Your childhood was leaving you. It is always a fretful time for the offspring of a child's imagination," answered Gilbert. "But we still continued to exist. We did not completely disappear."

"And now that I've started thinking about you again and using my imagination, you have returned to visit me, just like in old times."

Jamie screwed up his face in thought. "The imaginary friends who appeared when you imagined them," he said.

"Yes," said Persephone. "They became more and more real each day, so much so that one day they became incarnate and would visit me. Don't ask me how it happened. It just did."

"But there were others who saw us on our little visits, weren't there?" asked Robin.

"Oh, yes, the children of Nellie Brush, the old head housekeeper, and Billy Oakes, the young butler, who sadly lost his life at the Somme."

"Of course, we only ever visited in the flesh at Christmas, didn't we?" said Totty.

"In the flesh?" asked Jamie.

"Yes," said Benjamin. "All the other times that we were together with your grandmother throughout her childhood, we were present in spirit, so to speak."

"And tell me, please," said Persephone. "What have you been doing through all the years that we have been apart?"

"We have grown up and then grown old, just as you have," answered Hildegard with a degree of childlike naivety in her eyes.

"But what happened? I mean, where did you end up? Whom did you marry? Did you have any children?"

There was an unexpected silence. Blank expressions registered on all of their faces as if Persephone had turned the handle of a one-armed bandit that had come up trumps.

Totty looked down at the carpet, then gradually lifted her head upwards and moved closer to Persephone. Looking her in the eyes, she said, "You see, Persephone, we have had no lives since we stopped being your imaginary friends."

"Yes, Persephone, you simply stopped imagining. Although we existed, we had to wait on you to create the events that would have made our lives complete," said Robin.

Persephone looked at him, somewhat perplexed.

Marmaduke then spoke up. "We have just been waiting, waiting all those years for you to imagine for us again. Now that you have, we have come to visit you."

"I see," said Persephone with empathy.

"Yes, Persephone," said Maizie. "One reason we have come here on this particular Christmas Eve is to ask if you would please put the missing pieces together."

"I am an old woman now," explained Totty. " I have had a blissfully happy childhood but I was never a beautiful young woman who met her Prince Charming. I was never married or gave birth to any children."

"And I never had a wife whom I cherished," said Gilbert. "There was never anyone to love me in return. No family of my own. I was never to aspire to anything. Like Totty, I had a wonderful childhood and the memory is sacred. This has made me happy and balanced in old age but there are so many gaps in my life. Happenings that never were."

"I beg you, Persephone, please listen to us, your old friends. Please, try and imagine how our lives should have been, could have been, and fill in those painful empty spaces," pleaded Totty.

"Yes, all you have to do is imagine, just once more, as you used to do. Just imagine," said Marmaduke.

"Take away the long years of waiting in some faceless, nameless station and give me and my relatives standing with you now happy lives, just as you created our most happy childhood," said Maizie.

"I was the youngest," said Benjamin. "Please give me the life and sweet memories that I surely deserve."

"Oh, dear, I think I`m going to break down. This is bringing it all back, the great happiness tinged by the empty years," said Hildegard with wet eyes.

"Oh, for goodness sake, don`t cry, please not now, not on Christmas Eve," begged Persephone. Jamie jumped off his seat, pulled a tissue out of a box on top of a bureau, and handed it to Hildegard.

"We all love you so much," said Totty "But please, make our Christmas dream come true and imagine how our lives should have been."

"Yes, all you have to do is imagine and all our lives will be complete," said Robin hopefully.

Persephone touched her lips and frowned. "I had no idea, really no idea, of what you had all gone through due to my lack of thought."

"We're not making you culpable. You were not to know," said Marmaduke.

"Very well," said Persephone as she breathed in and straightened her back. "This very day, Christmas Day, I shall imagine what you would have done: where you lived, which places you visited, whom you married and whatever else you would like. I promise that I will fill your lives to the full and make them as happy as possible."

"Oh, I always wanted to spend a summer on the Riviera," chirped Maizie hopefully in her squeaky voice.

Gilbert butted in excitedly on the heel of her last word. "And me, to visit all those Greek islands that you told us about, with their dazzling blue sea and dolphins."

"Yes, and I will make all that happen and more."

"Never mind the Riviera and all the rest," said Hildegard. "I`m going to sail around the world and run in the Olympics just like the Ancient Greeks."

Gilbert turned to her. "And it'll be so nice to return to our youth and be young again," he said.

The grandfather clock struck one o'clock. Jamie felt anxious, as Saint Nick had not yet appeared. He opened the curtains of the large window and looked carefully out onto the dark nooks and crannies of the festive snow scene outside. Hugs and kisses ensued as Persephone assured her old friends that her promises would be kept. There were more embraces and handshakes, and just a few tears, as they said their goodbyes at the great door and then made their way out, back into the bitter cold of the wee small hours.

As they walked down the steps, Benjamin turned around and, as an afterthought, said perkily, "Oh, and just one other small request. Do you think you could give us all a surname?"

Persephone nodded and smiled.

As they made their way back over the white lawn, they left Persephone and Jamie standing under the lintel of the doorway. The friends waved enthusiastically just before they wandered farther into the darkness and then out of sight. Persephone and Jamie watched from the window and the warmth of the drawing room. For a few brief, pensive moments, Persephone's thoughts turned away from Christmas and back to the endless sunny summer days of childhood, running along a deserted beach with Ulysses on a far-off Greek island, surrounded by the deep kline blue of the Aegean Sea. When she returned to her present self, she noticed that Jamie was no longer with her in the drawing room. She heard the thud of his bedroom door as it closed.

'Of course,' she thought. Santa Claus had not yet arrived but he would, and very soon too. She switched off the lights and made tracks to retire to bed.

* * *

A shimmering silver in the sunny blue sky hit the sparkling frost on the steps of High Hedge House. The thick snow on the lawn glistened in jubilation as the faint peal of church bells in the village proclaimed that Christmas Day had at last arrived. Pieces of torn, gaily-coloured Christmas paper lay scattered around the enormous tree in the hall, as its tinselled bows shook from the movement of those who ran hurriedly around it.

That Santa Claus, perhaps under the alias of Father Christmas or Saint Nick, surely must exist to encounter such an abundance of much-appreciated gifts under the tree was most prominent in Jamie's mind as he opened the remainder of his presents from Persephone. He quickly rummaged through the pages of a brightly coloured atlas that Dolly had given him.

"I thought I'd buy him something educational since he's now 12," she said. "Beautiful book that, mind, beautiful, so it is." She observed Jamie with affection. "Yes, he's 12 years old now but before you know it, he'll be a teenager dancing to The Beatles and all them. Then the next thing, he'll be middle-aged. Eee. Time's one for passing quickly. One minute you're crying in your cot, the next thing, before you know it, you're buried in that old churchyard. Oh dear..." She chuckled on a subdued note and then went to see to breakfast.

Jamie rummaged through the shreds of multi-coloured paper just in case a present or two hadn't yet been opened. Lo and behold, when he had all but given up hope, he came across three rather large gifts, tightly wrapped in red string. It surprised him that he had not come across them earlier but there they were, right under the bottom bough of the Christmas tree. Each of the parcels had a neat little tag attached to it. One was intended for Dolly, while another was for Persephone. The third bore the name *Jamie* on it. *Merry Christmas, Jamie. So nice to have met you at last. Always remember that every Christmas is special and never forget to make it so. Have a lovely day!*
Lots of best wishes

Underneath, in a variety of handwriting, were all the names of the imaginary friends.

Jamie unwrapped the gift immediately. Inside was a large illustrated book entitled *Making Things and How to Be Imaginative and Creative* as well as a box of paints, crayons, and drawing paper.

"This will certainly keep me busy for the rest of the hols," he said.

Persephone then opened her Christmas present. Inside was a large black fur hat pierced by a bejewelled hatpin. "Why, it`s so lovely," she said, "I shall wear it today."

"And what about Dolly?" asked Jamie. "Isn`t she going to open hers?"

"Of course she will. She`ll do that shortly, when she`s finished preparing breakfast. We`ll just have a light snack today or we won`t have room for our Christmas dinner."

"And what are we going to have for that?" asked Jamie.

"Oh, why, we have roast goose with stewed apples, ham, chestnuts, and all sorts."

"And Christmas pudding?"

"Why, certainly, and plenty of it too, and there`s mince pies and Scotch trifle."

"I can`t wait," said Jamie.

"But you`ll have to. Waiting on it is all part of the fun, and then it all tastes even better."

"Why did they leave a present for Dolly?"

"Because they also know her."

"Has she met them, then?"

"Yes, she has."

"But I thought you said that Elsie Brush and her children saw them, didn`t you?"

"Yes, that`s right. Elsie was Dolly`s mother. She worked for my grandparents for many years."

"So has Alf seen *the friends* as well?"

"No, no, he hasn`t. Dolly and Alf will be having Christmas dinner with us, as they do every year. Then Dolly will go away for two weeks to stay with relatives in Cornwall."

Jamie burst open an inviting selection box and quickly devoured a bar of Cadbury`s. Persephone looked at him with the intention to scold but felt she couldn`t and certainly not on Christmas Day.

"Don`t eat too many of them or you won`t enjoy your Christmas dinner. Keep your selection boxes until Boxing Day and the days following it," she said but stopped at that. "Now go and get ready for matins. I`ve left your tie and white shirt on your bed. We`ll have some tea and toast and then go."

"It`s all ready!" shouted Dolly from the breakfast room. This was followed by a rather off-tune festal chorus: "*O, come all ye faithful, joyful and triumphant…*"

* * *

Alf drove the dilapidated old limousine up to the steps of the great door as Jamie looked out of the drawing room window, dressed in his grey suit, partly made up of shorts, since he was not yet of age to wear long trousers. It was a snug fit that his mother had chosen for him on a shopping trip to New York. His white shirt had been neatly pressed by Dolly, and she had helped him tie a proper "*man`s*" knot in his red silk tie. Persephone had insisted on him putting Brylcream in his hair but had backed down after Dolly had vehemently stated that it was *not the fashion these days.*

Alf entered the great hallway. "And a merry Christmas to you, my dear!" he said to Dolly.

She smiled and returned his wishes while shaking his hand warmly.

"Any chance of a quick hot cup of tea? It`s cold outside."

"Of course there is. I`ve already made you a pot. It`s on the kitchen table. Help yourself," said Dolly.

Alf walked over the hallway to the stairs leading to the kitchen.

"I wish Merry Christmas and make tea only for them that wipes their feet!" said Dolly as she pointed to a great clump of snow on the carpet.

Jamie continued to inspect his new Christmas gifts for a further 15 minutes until Persephone came downstairs. She entered the room dressed in her black fur coat and diamond earrings, in which she, her mother, and her grandmother had been married. Her head was covered by the hat gifted to her that very morning by *the friends*. As she looked at Jamie, she said, "How smart you look today. You know, you so resemble my dear brother Ulysses." She felt her large heart fill with emotion and then she spontaneously bent down and hugged him tightly, her soft fur hat squeezing against his cheeks.

Jamie picked up the book given to him by the friends and opened it. "I must learn how to be imaginative and creative," he said.

"Indeed but that is something that you do not learn. It`s something that just grows within you and can become very powerful."

"The friends, they came about because you imagined them. Like magic, I suppose."

"Something like that but more than that. You know, Jamie, often when people grow up and become adults, and even when they grow old, there is a part of them that never changes, a part that is still a child. Often, childhood dreams and games can almost be brought to life, and maybe only occasionally, through some sort of mystery, they can turn into a reality of sorts. It`s something that transcends all logic and reason. An author creates a play through imagination, and its characters come to life through actors, but perhaps the characters of imagination, the imaginary friends, do not really need actors to give them life. On Christmas Eve, when a mystical, magical serenity descends over the world, they may appear in flesh. Logic. What is logic? Why, it`s just another man-made creation." She put her arms around Jamie's shoulders. He closed his eyes and took on a countenance of sheer concentration.

"I wish today would never end and that it will be today forever," he said. Then he reopened his eyes.

"Eyes are a beautiful gift," said Persephone.

"I agree," said Jamie in response.

Alf came into the hall. He was sporting his good tie, which had been taken out of the wardrobe year after year for umpteen weddings and Christmas Days. He sported a black Crombie coat that had started to wear at the collar. Dolly appeared, having discarded her long white apron and cap for a large navy picture hat and a camel coat

"Everyone ready?" asked Alf. "Let`s go!"

Persephone picked up Jamie`s Harris Tweed coat and handed it to him. "You`ll need this!"

The three of them left the house and walked briskly down the snow-topped steps. Dolly linked her arm with Persephone`s to guide her and then they all jumped into the car. Alf started the engine and drove it cautiously through the icy country lanes surrounded by snow-capped trees, hedges, and the white roofs of old thatched cottages.

Jamie turned to his grandmother. "This is such a special Christmas. I believe this is my best Christmas ever," he said.

"That`s because High Hedge House is a very special place," said Persephone "A very, very special place."

* * *

Chapter 3

ACROSS THE WATER

Things were difficult for the Kennedy family after Dad lost his job at the factory. Scott had felt an unease around the home in the days and weeks that followed. His father, who had been nurtured on a strict work ethic, had found the whole affair degrading and sank into a mild depression, which had made him testy and awkward. In those days, men would never admit to such problems for fear of appearing weak. There had been plenty of contracts to be undertaken by Swain's, the company he had been employed by, but the directors had decided to move the plant to Darwin, where for some reason, it was going to be financially viable. Dad had worked there since the family's early days in Australia. He had been on a reasonable wage, so the whole affair had disrupted a series of family plans such as holidays and moving home. Mum had taken on a chain of cleaning jobs which ranged from the grandiose dwellings of the newly rich to hoovering and scrubbing the carpets of the local bank and The West's Olympia and Metro cinemas, which she gave a good going-over at the crack of dawn. She had returned home exhausted, which had lead to a spate of "light teas," i.e., boiled eggs or simple salads, for the evening meal. It was a relief for both his father and his mother when Dad had eventually found more gainful employment in early October and the overall atmosphere at home improved greatly. Scott's eldest sister, Sheena, had also taken on a Saturday job at a local department store, the wages from which provided her with clothes and other accessories for the fashion-conscious teenager. The winter had been grim but the days were turning from pleasantly warm to extremely hot as the Southern Hemisphere veered towards its summer. Indeed, summer in Australia was as much a true summer as summer could ever be, with days by the beach or swimming in the pool and the sun ever shining and reliant. Scott, however, still missed his old school friends and his relatives back in Angus, and in particular his grandmother, who was now very old. He corresponded with them still, if only on a sporadic basis. The summer holidays and Christmas approached but Scott still missed the rich, dark winter afternoons and soft, bright snow of a Christmas in Scotland. That was one reason he had never really felt that much of an Australian. His father and Sheena had taken to the continent like ducks to water, and his only other brother, Greg, had immersed himself totally in Australian life and culture, becoming an avid fan of cricket and playing on the local team. Mum, on the other hand, had found it somewhat hard to adapt to life in her new country and clung on as best she could to her native culture by getting involved in Caledonian clubs and country dancing classes and clinging with grim death to the old Scots customs that surrounded Christmas and New Year.

Scott's maternal Auntie Marian and her husband, Uncle Sye, along with their only daughter, Reena, had emigrated to Perth in 1962. Scott had been very close to these particular relatives and, as a small child, had felt baffled and bewildered when they had decided to take the bull by the horns and embark on the journey to a new and possibly better life Down Under. The entire extended family had arranged a lavish party on the night before their departure. At the end of the soiree, old Auntie Kitty had played a rendition of Waltzing Matilda on the piano. All had joined in and heartily sung. Curious as to where this Australia place was, Scott had asked his Auntie Marion, "Where is Australia? Is it far away?"

"Oh, yes, it's very far away," Marian informed him

"It's far across the water," Uncle Sye added.

'Across the water,' thought Scott.

Scott missed them. He was very fond of his aunt's home-baked cakes, which would cover the table when they visited for tea. And then there were the Cadbury's chocolate bars that she always brought him when they would visit his home.

Some weeks after they had gone off to Australia, and only a couple of weeks before Christmas, Scott's pleasant memories of his relatives led him to stand on the shore of the River Tay, just east of Dundee. After all, Uncle Sye had informed him that it was far across the water, and so Scott stood and looked over to Tayport in Fife, which lay directly on the other side of the river: "across the water." It seemed so logical to a five-year-old that Tayport must be Australia. He focused his eyes and peered over to Fife to try and catch a glimpse of his *Australian* relatives.

Australia was a part of the world that, some years later, he was to find his own self in after his parents had decided to follow his aunt and uncle and immigrate to Oz. While Marion and Sye had settled in Perth, Scott's family was domiciled in Semaphore, a modest area of Adelaide in a Welsh enclave that also hosted a number of Greeks. While Auntie Marion and Uncle Sye had initially lived in Perth, they had moved, with a promise of highly paid employment, to Darwin in the Northern Territory, which was hundreds of miles from Adelaide and a place where it remained hot all year round. This resulted in there being no reunion with the relatives due to distance. However, they lived in patient expectation that they would all get together in the near future.

Advent quickly passed into its final days and the Kennedys prepared to celebrate yet another Australian Christmas basking in strong sunshine and high temperatures.

Sheena had been dealt a severe blow to her Christmas spending when she lost her job at the department store, having been sacked when she was asked, by a customer, for an honest opinion on how she suited a dress she had tried on. Sheena, brutally honest as always, had told her in all sincerity that she looked like mutton dressed as lamb and that people would only laugh behind her back if she were stupid enough to purchase the dress. It seemed that the last thing the customer wanted was the truth. She had rushed off in a flush of anger and complained in no uncertain terms to the manageress.

Mum, determined to celebrate Christmas as she saw proper, scanned the supermarket shelves for the exact ingredients for festive fare. She also made frequent visits to the Scottish butchers and bakers. One reason Mum wanted to move house was that the family's current dwelling lacked modern air conditioning and relied on old-fashioned fans that spun at high speed from the ceiling. Greg had an important cricket match on Christmas morning and a friend had invited Sheena over to her family's swimming pool.

As December continued, the temperatures soared and Mum was spending more time than usual in the kitchen, stirring the ingredients of her much-complimented Christmas cake, rolling marzipan, and creating the shortbread pastry with which she made her mince pies. "Since it's so hot, aren't you going to have a nice salad for Christmas dinner this year?" Greg asked her as she opened a fresh jar of mincemeat.

"Salad? Salad? For Christmas dinner? Why, that's something you eat on Boxing Day. I could never hold my head high again when I go into town knowing that I had dished up salad to you lot on Christmas Day." "Well, how about salad with turkey instead of Brussels sprouts? Mrs Dimitrikopoulou three doors down gave you the recipe for her Greek salad last year, remember? Why don't you do that?"

"Nice though her Greek salad may be, it's not what I'd have for Christmas dinner. Tradition counts for something."

The windows of the Kennedys' living room reflected the festive season in Northern Europe, with white snow having been sprayed over them in an attempt to make the family feel more at home. There was, however, no need to spray white snow onto the glass panes that particular year, as the snow from the previous year was still imprinted on the glass. Mum had tried unsuccessfully on several occasions to wash it off. They had remained in a semi-permanent state of Christmas all year round.

"I must dab some bleach on that and see if it won't come off. I've tried everything. It gives people a bad impression of the place if they pass and see all that. The neighbours might think I haven't bothered to clean the windows since last Christmas," Mum fretted to Dad.

Not taking the issue as seriously as Mum, he responded by saying, "Instead of going to all the trouble of cleaning it off, why don`t you just keep up the Christmas tree and decorations all year round? Then we wouldn`t have to do anything come December every year."

"Oh, ha-ha, how funny, but may I remind you that you live here as well? It`s in your interest that we live in a respectable household. That reminds me, remember to get a couple of bottles of whisky for Hogmanay when you go out tomorrow. I`ll leave that aspect of things up to you but mind and get something decent. I don`t mind how much it costs. We don`t want people saying that they had been handed cheap whisky at our place at New Year."

Dad smiled mischievously to himself. "Don`t you worry. I`ll see if I can get a good malt."

Mum had always found Hogmanay the hardest night of the year. At the stroke of midnight, she had run out into the backyard with tears in her eyes as the bells chimed while fireworks went off and Auld Lang Syne was sung over Australia

The Kennedys' former neighbour, Mrs Mathews, called in for a fleeting visit on the morning of Christmas Eve. The Mathews had made a decent amount of money from the garage they had owned and had bought a "little bungalow" in Modbury. Mum said that Mrs Mathews had acquired all these airs and graces since moving and she didn`t have much time for her. However, it was Christmas, so Mum tried to be kind and welcoming even though she knew that the main point of Mrs Mathews' visit was to brag about her upward mobility.

Mum handed Mrs Mathews a cup of tea and offered her a plate full of freshly baked mince pies, of which she was very proud.

"Delicious, of course," Mrs Mathews said as she bit into the shortbread pastry. Mum felt her heart swell.

Mrs Mathews swallowed the piece of pie and then said, "And may I ask what you are having for Christmas dinner?"

"Oh, for us it`s going to be good old turkey, roast spuds, and Brussels. Our Christmas dinners never vary."

"Oh, really. This year we're having some expensive crayfish and the best prawns that the fishmonger has on offer. And I thought we could have that Greek salad, remember, the recipe that Mrs Dimitrikopoulou gave us? I went to a Greek delicatessen in Adelaide and bought the best quality feta to put in the salad. It wasn't cheap but it is Christmas and it's not as if we can't afford it."

"It's so nice you've got your own little place in Modbury. I'd love to own my own home."

"Well, I must confess, it is rather a thrill to have such a lovely place with such a nice garden. We're considering moving to North Brighton or Glenelg. We just need to find that perfect little place. We viewed a lovely villa in Glenelg just the other week. I suppose it's just that some people get on in life and move on and other people ... er ... just stay where they are."

Dad came into the living room as they were chatting

"And how nice to see you again after such a long time. How are things doing in Modbury?"

"Mrs Mathews and I were just talking about owning our own home. She was just saying how well she's done."

"And good luck to you, that's what I say. Nice to see you're a lady of leisure now. It's far cry from when you had to scrub the floors of the local supermarket when you and your husband first came to Australia"

"Yes ... well ... that was some years ago now."

"Where does the time go? That's what I ask myself. What have you got lined up for tonight? Anything special?" Mrs Kennedy asked.

"Well, we're going to Saint George's for the service. They're having Handel's Halleluia Chorus this year."

"Oh, the choir is singing the Halleluia Chorus, are they?" Dad said

"Oh, no, not the choir, Mr. Kennedy."

"Not the choir? Then who?"

"Why, I am singing the Halleluia Chorus tonight!"

"You mean you're singing with the choir?" asked Mum.

"No, Mrs Kennedy, it is I who will be singing the whole Halleluia Chorus."

Mum and Dad looked at each other in surprise.

"You're singing it all on your own?" Mum asked in disbelief.

"Yes, I am. I've always been somewhat talented musically."

Mum and Dad glanced at each other, speechless. Out of politeness, they refrained from commenting.

Mrs Mathews picked up another mince pie and popped it into her mouth. "These are really scrummy," she said.

* * *

Mum had gone with Scott and Sheena to the watchnight service at the Scots Church on North Terrace in Adelaide. Greg had given them a lift in his second-hand blue Ford, which he had recently purchased and was very proud of, so much so that he polished it with elbow grease every day till it gleamed brightly in the summer sun. As the car passed the shores of the Le Fevre Peninsula, Scott stated that his favourite day was Christmas Day but that the 24th came in a very close second. Mrs Kennedy's face assumed a reminiscent gaze as they drove further along the coast.She turned to Scott.

"You know, when my parents were children in the early 1900s and the last part of the 19th century, they celebrated Christmas Day on January 6th. That was the date of the old Christmas in Scotland."

"Old Christmas?" asked a surprised Sheena.

"Yes, I think at one point they changed the calendars and the date in the new calendar was December 24th."

"Well, I never knew that. Imagine having to wait another two weeks before you got any presents," Scott said.

Greg drove the car on through Christmas Eve and farther towards home.

The old familiar carols now sung, they felt that Christmas was now, at least, partly complete. Only the following day's feast and merriment remained to make it totally Christmas. When they arrived home, Mum served up some glasses of chilled homemade lemonade from the fridge and some of her very special homemade mince pies. The family dived into them mercilessly and consumed them all quickly, one after the other.

The family always looked forward to the annual serving up of Mum's mince pies. The recipe was a guarded secret that she never revealed to anyone. Mrs Mathews had been trying for years to get Mum to reveal her secret but to no avail. The scrumptious pastry coated in sugar complimented the rich mincemeat inside.

"Ah! Perfect!" Scott said after he had eaten his fourth.

"The taste of Christmas," Greg remarked as he gulped down the cooling lemonade after eating his fair share.

"Well, it's getting late and I've got an early appointment with the kitchen tomorrow," Mum said as she made tracks to retire.

"And I've got an important match tomorrow but that follows my opening of the presents," Greg said.

"I'll leave a clean cozy out for you for when you go swimming tomorrow," Mum shouted to Sheena from the top of the stairs.

After the others had all gone upstairs, and just before he went to bed, Scott stood at the window and looked over to the ocean as it bathed in the moonlight. He softly hummed the tune to Silent Night as he thought of his Christmases back in Angus and of all his old friends including how, on Christmas Eve, they had always called round to his grandmother to exchange presents. He thought about how far away all that was now and how he so much wanted those Christmases to return. For several minutes, he felt sad.

Mum came back into the room. "Are you alright? It's time you were in bed. Why are you standing here in the dark?"

"Oh, nothing," Scott said. "I'm just thinking of the Christmases back home. I mean, Christmas is fine here in Semaphore but it's … I don't know … not the same. I still miss everyone so much. Even the TV here is full of repeats at Christmas and there are very few Christmas specials."

"I always used to enjoy Christmas Night with the Stars on the BBC back home," Mum said as she put her arm over his shoulder and, although having similar pangs in her heart, tried to dispel his negativity. "Oh, you've just got a bout of homesickness. It'll soon pass. You know, I still miss all the folks back home and everything back in Scotland. In fact, I miss it every day. But your dad loves it here and so do Sheena and Greg, so I try to think of all the beautiful aspects of Australia when I get homesick. We really must think of Australia as our home now even though our hearts may still be in Angus."

Scott listened to his mother's words, then went upstairs. After all, tomorrow would be special. It would be Christmas Day.

The night of that Christmas Eve was a restless one for the family, not in anticipation and excitement for Santa's visit but for being far above average temperature-wise for summer. Mrs Kennedy found it nigh impossible to sleep, so she got up and had a cold shower in the early hours. "I can't wait till we move to a more modern house with decent air conditioning," she said to her husband as she returned to bed. The old-fashioned fans whisked around on the ceiling above as she managed to slowly fall into a deep, overdue slumber.

"Santa Claus" had visited during the night and left presents for all, including for Mr and Mrs Kennedy. As was usual, Santa's glass of whisky, filled right to the brim, was empty by morning.

"I'm sure Santa would much prefer a cool glass of Coca-Cola now that we live in Australia. The poor old soul must be sweating after all that whisky he drinks at our place every year," Mrs Kennedy said sarcastically as she passed Dad his morning coffee.

Sheena had opened a parcel to find a brand-new turquoise bikini inside. "Oh, what a lovely colour! I've been admiring one exactly like that in Flanagan's shop window for weeks."

"We know," Dad said as he smiled wryly.

"You see, I did tell you a clean cozy would be waiting for you!" Mum chuckled.

"I'll wear it when I go round to Ruth's pool later," Sheena said, happy and content.

Mrs Kennedy made an early start in the kitchen, just as she had planned.

After a coffee and a slice of toast, Mrs Kennedy dressed in her best pinafore apron, which itself had been a Christmas present from a previous year. In no time, the turkey had been stuffed and was slowly cooking in the oven, as were a number of other accompanying dishes. Vegetables boiled furiously on all four rings of the cooker. Mrs Kennedy had also spent part of the morning making Skirlie, a traditional recipe from the Northeast of Scotland, made from oatmeal, onions, and oil, which her grandmother had taught her to make when she was a girl. Grandmother's recipes often included oats as an ingredient, which took them far from the porridge of the breakfast table. There had been oats in scones, pancakes, omelettes, and fried fish. Greg had gone off in his blue Ford, which had made a noisy contribution to Christmas morning due to his revving up the car engine in youthful boldness. Sheena had gone over to her friend Ruth's to swim in her family pool and Mum had thrust a box of sweets into her hand as a present for Ruth's mum. "Seeing it's Christmas," she said as she did so. As the morning went on, Mrs Kennedy, firmly inhabiting the kitchen, opened a large biscuit tin on a shelf, in which were kept the mince pies. She took one out and ate it, then put her hand back into the tin and took out another, which she consumed just as quickly. She then reached up to the cupboard above the sink and took down an already opened bottle of cheap sherry, which she had used as part of the ingredients for the trifle prepared the day before. She now whisked the fresh cream with a Kenwood Chefette and added it to the set custard before she continued to decorate the surface of the trifle with a pattern made up of fresh fruit and hundreds and thousands that she had copied from Fanny Craddock off a BBC Christmas cookery show she had watched some years before. Mum poured a tiny amount of sherry into a glass and smiled as it soothingly trickled down her throat. Then, just like with the mince pies, she helped herself to another sherry but this time, feeing exhausted and stressed from the heat and the morning's work in the kitchen, she filled the glass to the brim as the old, faulty fan spun round above her, sticking and then jolting as it did so. The heat outside had risen in potency, and as the potatoes and other root vegetables came to a boil, the steam from the plum duff gifted its temperature to the existing Fahrenheit in the room. As if the heat wasn't bad enough, the roof fan above suddenly spun round at a terrible rate, then made a loud clicking sound, and then abruptly stopped. Mum plodded on regardless, determined to have Christmas dinner ready for when Greg and Sheena returned, which would be soon. Scott amused himself outside in the shade with some of the presents that had awaited him on the living room floor. Finding it hard to cope with the enormity of her task, Mum took another few sips of the sherry and followed it up with a big tumbler of tap water. She could hear the outside door open; it was Sheena returning from her swim at Ruth's. A few minutes later, Greg arrived back from his cricket match, elated because his team had won. Mr Kennedy, who had gone for a Christmas morning stroll, came into the kitchen and threw a paper bag onto the table.

"What's that?" Mum asked.

"Oh, it's just some fresh prawns that I bought. I thought we could have them as a starter."

"But I've already made…" Mum said before Dad interrupted.

"Yes, I know but it's Christmas and I'm sure we'll all have room inside for a bit more."

At that, the potatoes started boiling over and Mum ran to turn them off. Then she opened the oven to take out the by-now well-cooked bird, and the heat in the room soared.

"God's truth, this place is like a sauna in here! It's terrible!" said Greg as he entered the room.

"That bloody roof fan's kaput. Trust it to go on a day like today," Dad said as they made their way out of the kitchen.

"I'll give you a hand in there," said Sheena.

"Yes, you just enjoy the food and let us women do all the hard work!" Mrs Kennedy said with just a hint of annoyance.

"Typical men! Oh, it`s so hot in here, it`s unbearable," Sheena added.

On hearing the noise of smashing dishes, Greg ran back into the kitchen only to see poor old Mum lying flat on the floor. "Are you alright? he shouted in a panic.

Scott ran into the kitchen. "What`s happened?" he asked, aghast.

Mr Kennedy tried to help his wife back up onto her feet. He turned round to Greg. "Give her a glass of that cooking sherry stuff," he said.

Greg looked at the bottle. "It looks as if Mum`s already been at it. There`s hardly any left."

Sheena dabbed a cold, damp facecloth on Mrs Kennedys' brow as she came round to consciousness once more

"Och, it`s an awfy hit i here an yon bloomin` fan isnae ony guid, Foo did it hae tae brack the day o awe days?fit kin I dae!" she exclaimed as she lapsed back into her native Doric-Scots tongue.

With the meal cooked, the family sat down at the table and tucked into their traditional Christmas lunch, which they heartily enjoyed with silent appreciation for Mrs Kennedys' wonderful culinary skills.

"That was absolutely delicious, Mum. I`m so full I can hardly move. But I ... er ... do think that maybe next year you should try something a bit more Australian. I mean, the whole thing would be a lot less stressful and a lot easier." murmered Greg lethargically.

"Yes, look what happened today. You passed out with the heat – a combination of the high temperatures, the faulty fan, and the steam and heat coming from the cooker. Maybe next year we could think more along the lines of fish or more seafood," Dad said in a concerned but tactful tone.

"Or we could even have our Christmas dinner on the beach. That would be great!" Sheena stated perkily.

"Yes, yes, but I know you`ve all truly enjoyed today`s feast, as I know you do every Christmas Day, and I`ll continue to keep Christmas as I think fit. I mean, when we move and get a place with proper air conditioning, everything will be different, so things won`t be changing."

The family smiled contentedly.

After dinner, Scott put on his swimming trunks and T-shirt, took some mince pies outside, and walked along the beach on the Gulf Saint Vincent coastline near his home. He saw some of his new school friends, who, happy to see him, beckoned him over to their company. The boys, like Scott, were all in a festive, happy mood. Scott looked at the ocean as the bright summer sun shone down on it, endowing it with a silvery, golden countenance. The many attractive bright poinsettias in their sheer redness bestowed a beguiling façade to the whole scene. He had never, in fact, noticed its unique beauty before. The negativity and melancholy he had felt the previous night were gone. Although part of him remained in Scotland, and always would, he now accepted that his real home was Australia in all its awesome, natural wonder. It was on that Christmas Day that Scott became a true Australian.

Chapter 4

THE ROAD HOME

The bells of the cathedral pealed out in their own expression of heavenly jubilation as I walked down the snow-decked steps. They were not in the slightest bit slippery, and the snow oozed with winter's freshness. The atmosphere, in its renowned mysterious activity, had proven the weather forecasters wrong. They had forecast a rainy Christmas but at exactly five minutes past midnight, the dome of the cathedral had felt the first touch of a snowflake. Like so many Christmases before, going back generations, the dome of the cathedral was soon covered in its blanched mantle. By the last carol at Midnight Mass, the snow had started to fall heavily and coat the cathedral's body in the icing-like beauty that promoted it to the position of a Christmas card cover. I had decided to attend Christmas Eve's Midnight Mass at the last minute and had driven into town in around thirty minutes. I did, however, manage to arrive a good five minutes before the first carol, during which several latecomers piled in discreetly. The drive into the city of Deeburgh had been quiet and uneventful. I was surprised and even delighted to see very little traffic on the night roads, despite the promises of the city's festive lights. Midnight Mass was touched by the odd mixture of festive cheer, by those who classed Christmas as a joyous occasion, a celebration of peace and goodwill, and a serious solemnity by those who classed it as one of the church's most solemn celebrations and whose faces wore the required frowns of their interpretation of Christmas. The two expectations of Christmas were, of course, entirely different bed partners and lived together, on Christmas Eve, this the holiest night of nights, in an uneasy silent stillness. It was now the early hours of Christmas Day. I left the cathedral's immediate vicinity and walked towards my car, which I had parked on Cross Street. I hoped that the roads back home would not be too treacherous due to the sudden bout of winter weather.

Treacherous road conditions due to inclement weather had more often than not put me off from setting out to Midnight Mass. It was, in many ways, a sort of pilgrimage to a childhood that lay somewhere in a Christmas past still clinging to a vague Medieval connection to my normal, daily life. The snow began to fall less heavily and I looked up into the deep darkness of the late December sky, like a child searching for a glimpse of Santa Claus as the evening wound on monotonously slowly until bedtime. That Christmas Eve was never the same again upon the revelation of Santa's true whereabouts was indeed and very much an understatement. I had often wished that my current state of belief in the saint could be revived.

As I put my key into the ignition, I realised that no more flakes were falling on my windscreen and that the snowfall had stopped, perhaps endowing us with just enough to turn the streets and landscape into something truly festive and fill the hearts of the populace with a joyful pang, rather than that of hardship and inconvenience that a continuous period of harsh weather would create. The roads outside of the metropolis were by no means hazardous, though I drove carefully, as the road forked eastwards, into the initial wizened foliage of the countryside. A few late-night revellers clung defensively to the narrow, grassy paths that lined the main roads as they walked home from revelrous activity. I turned off on the left of the main road, across from the Northway Bridge, and drove into the narrow side road that led into Duneffy. Its tiny picturesque hamlets clustered around small fields like insecure children afraid of being parted from their parents. Few lights still shone from living room windows. Most of the windows were dark, their owners having long fallen into sleep. Beyond them lay fields, bare and unwelcoming, their trees like skeletons with white snow replacing greenery, hung on the dark branches. Soon, no sign of any life could be seen and the snow that blanketed the fields blended in with the black winter's night, scraggy and wild in its bleakness. As I turned the sharp corner at Moothill, two ladies wearing black woollen shawls waved my car down. I slowed my engine, stopped, and opened the window, wondering if they were in some peril.

"So sorry to trouble you but we`ve been walking home from Midnight Mass in Deeburgh. It`s so cold and we`ve been walking for some time. Would you please be so kind as to give us a lift home?"

"Of course I will. Where do you live?" There were two of them. One was in her thirties and the other, who looked like she was the first woman's mother, must have been in her late sixties.

"We live at Saracen House, on Duncan Avenue."

"Oh, yes, I know," I said.

Duncan Avenue was a village, just on the approach to Duneffy. It was an unusual place that consisted of one long elegant street of a dozen or so rather grand mansions surrounded by fields. I had passed it many a time and often envied its residents for their grandiose and elegant dwellings.

The two demure women smiled graciously but said very little. I was somewhat struck by their attire. They were wearing the Sunday best of thick black shawls of those in mourning, which were in vogue over fifty years ago or even more.

"Where did you attend Midnight Mass?" I asked.

"We`ve been to the cathedral," the eldest replied.

"We always go to the cathedral, always have done every Christmas for many years."

It struck me as a bit odd that they had attended Midnight Mass at the cathedral, yet they had walked all the way to Moothill corner and arrived there earlier than I, who had driven the same distance. The younger woman lowered her eyes coyly but did not speak. She pulled her thick shawl farther over her head as the dark night hid her face and the powdered white sugar of the fields whizzed on behind us.

We drove onto Duncan Avenue. "Which one is it?" I enquired.

"It`s the third house on the left," replied the older woman. "This one here with the high gates?"

I drove through the large iron gates, which were already wide open. On the left gate post, highlighted by the car lights, was written "Saracen House." The gateway led to a long drive, lined by handsome spruce trees now white with the recent snowfall. A clumsy Gothic

Victorian edifice of red sandstone stood in a dominant position at the end. A number of steps ascended to the authoritarian-looking door, flanked by Doric columns on each side. Above, a circular window encased a display of stained glass. Due to the darkness of the night, its depiction was hard to decipher. It had been briefly illuminated by the front lights of my car as I parked on the gravel at the foot of the steps.

I turned around to the two women in the back seat. "Well, here we are," I said with a smile.

"Oh, thank you so much. We really are most grateful for your assistance. Isn`t that so, Isabelle?" said the eldest woman.

"Oh, yes, it was so bitterly cold on the way back from the cathedral," said the youngest. It was the first time she`d spoken since she`d been in the car.

"You are really more than welcome. After all, it is Christmas Eve, is it not? I always say, if you can`t help a stranger on Christmas Eve ... well..."

"Quite!" said the eldest woman.

"But, were you not afraid?" I asked as an afterthought. "Were you two not afraid to wave down a car at such a late hour? Weren`t you just a little hesitant?"

"No, not at all," said the eldest jovially. "We can look after ourselves. Nothing frightens us, does it, Isabelle?"

The younger woman giggled. "No, Mother, nothing at all."

"Since you have done us a kindness and, as you say, it is Christmas Eve, may we offer you a brandy before you continue your journey?"

"Please accept our invitation. You have done us a favour and it`s such a cold night," said Isabelle.

"Alright then, that would be very nice."

We walked up the snow-covered steps towards the formidable door. The older woman inserted the key into the keyhole.

"By the way, my name is Mrs Osbourne and this is my daughter, Isabelle," she said.

I nodded. 'Just as I had thought,' I said to myself.

Once inside the hall, already lit by the flames of candles burning in two candelabras, Mrs Osbourne picked up a heavy single candlestick filled with a long white wax candle and leant its wick against a flame from the candelabra. "This way," she said and led us up a spiral staircase.

The flame from the single candle flickered as we walked upstairs. It cast shadows against the walls and gave life to the rows of paintings: portraits and landscapes that lined the ascent to the first floor. I imagined that the portraits were most likely some of the Osbournes' antecedents. On the landing of the first floor, a double door opened into a most elaborate living room, its floor covered in a thick shag pile carpet. The velvet curtains had heavy pelmets laced with crystal drops that glistened as they hung in the candlelight. Yet another pair of candelabras was perched on heavy oak sideboards covered in an abundance of crochet runners and doilies. Mrs Osbourne lit the fire in the hearth with the help of the single candle. Housed within its intricately carved oak mantelpiece, it soon began to crackle and burn. Between the window and the hearth, a Christmas tree that must have been ten feet tall sparkled in all its eloquent finery as Mrs Osbourne carefully lit each of the tiny wax candles in their peglike bases, which Isabelle helped to hold until all were alight and the glorious tree exuded a very Christmassy glow. The cold room began to feel cosy as the blazing fire in the hearth stretched its warm hands into the four corners of the room. A festive glow soon touched all parts of the room from the window to the ceiling, from the floor to the door. I settled down onto a comfortable armchair and relaxed back into its soft cushions as Mrs Osbourne poured a large brandy from a decanter, which Isabelle promptly brought over to me. It looked like an idyllic Christmas Eve scene, yet I had some inexplicable, uneasy feeling that something was not totally in order. With the light from the many candles and the fireside glow, I could now see the faces of the two women much more clearly. Isabelle had long brown hair and a sallow face with deep-set, rather attractive eyes that sparkled. They were complimented further by large, spider-like eyelashes. Her mother had a strong aristocratic nose with a wrinkled forehead and the salt and pepper hair of an ageing woman who had not yet turned completely grey. She had the same sparkle in her eyes, tinged with a glaze of wisdom and experience. She stood tall and graceful in old age.

"The choir sang so sweetly this evening at the cathedral," said Mrs Osbourne as she sat on the chair next to the hearth.

"They did indeed," I said. "It brought back memories of when I used to sing in the church choir when I was just about ten or eleven."

"You know, I've always loved singing Christmas carols, ever since I was a little girl. I always say there's nothing so beautiful as a carol," said Mrs Osbourne. She grinned and then laughed gently.

I looked upwards. "I must say, you certainly have the place looking most festive," I said as I noticed boughs of thick, prickly, green holly that hung from the ceiling.

"Oh, my family has always kept Christmas as best we could. We like to take as much as we can out of the Christmas season until there is not a drop of it left by Twelfth Night," said Mrs Osbourne. She turned once again to her daughter. "Isn't that so, Isabelle?"

There was a slight silence before she eventually replied. "Indeed it is, Mother. No one quite celebrates the birth of Christ like we do. Indeed, no one."

I felt comfortable in the armchair as the coal fire crackled and sparked in its hearth. I couldn't help but notice how "old world" everything was but it did add a touch of quintessential Christmas tradition to the place.

I had been there over an hour when I looked at the hands of the clock. "I really must go. Look at the time!"

"May I offer you one more brandy before you leave?" asked Mrs Osbourne.

"Oh, yes, do stay and have just one more, or perhaps you would rather have a coffee, since you are driving," pleaded Isabelle.

"Oh, no, I'm afraid I really must go. You two must be very tired yourselves," I said.

"Oh, no, we never tire easily and we never really need much sleep, do we Isabelle?" asked Mrs Osbourne.

"Indeed, we don`t," said Isabelle. She once again smiled pleasantly as she brought me my coat.

"Thank you again," said Mrs Osbourne. "Now that you are acquainted with us and know where we live, you must come and visit us again sometime," she said with a swelling of warmth in the last few words.

"We are always at home on Sunday afternoons. You are most welcome to call, heartily welcome," said Isabelle.

"Do see the gentleman out, Isabelle," said her mother. "And a merry Christmas to you," she added.

"A merry Christmas to both of you. I would very much like to call sometime in the New Year," I said. I left Mrs Osbourne standing graciously beside the Christmas tree, her hand on a string of pearls that hung around her throat. I put on my coat and Isabelle accompanied me downstairs and back to the main door. Isabelle did not reply but simply smiled in a shy, almost flirtatious manner, then closed the door.

"Thank you for the brandy. Good night," I said. Then I walked down the steps and opened the car door. I stopped momentarily and looked up at the living room window, which was illuminated in the darkness by the candlelight. 'Almost another world,' I thought to myself. I climbed into my car, turned the ignition key, and drove up the pitch-black drive, away from Saracen House, back through the high iron gates, which were wide open, and onto the silence of the deserted main road.

Christmas Eve piety and Christmas Day overindulgence soon gave way to the bells of New Year and a chilly January with dull, overcast grey skies to go with it. The newspapers had reported that January was the most depressing month given that the festive season was gone and still plenty of cold, dark days lay ahead.

On a Sunday afternoon in late January, I was driving back to Duneffy after having visited friends in Deeburgh. It was still daylight but dusk`s husky haze had already started to compete with the remainder of the day. I happened to drive along Duncan Avenue and it came into my mind that it might be a polite gesture to drop in to visit the two ladies to whom I had given a lift on Christmas Eve or, rather, the wee small hours of Christmas morning. I drove up the salubrious, well-kept avenue lined with pristine villas but could not for the life of me see Saracen House. I drove back, up and down it again, but still no sign of Saracen House, so I parked my car, walked up the avenue, and inspected each of the houses as I passed them. I unexpectedly came across an old, rusty gate that had thick bracken and other wild bushes growing out of it, with an overgrown driveway thick with foliage and wild grass. Then I noticed, between sprawling spruce trees on the side of a crumbling gate post, still legible, the name Saracen House. It had certainly been extremely dark on Christmas Eve and there was a fair degree of snow and frost on the driveway and, yes, there had been a few elegant spruce trees but nothing like the unruly, neglected mess of overgrown bushes and weeds. Everything, if I could remember rightly, had been very pristine and landscaped, in keeping with the other villas in the area. The name on the gatepost had stood out in clear, crisp gold carved letters, yet there seemed to be no doubt that this was the very gateway I had driven through. I stroked the hard, brown, flaky rust of the gate as if to test its authenticity. There were certainly no other entrances on the avenue that bore the name of Saracen House. Several of the other mansions had been divided into flats, yet Saracen House was still occupied as one single entity, or it had been when I had drank brandy with the ladies. I squeezed through an opening in the immobile gate, which was stiff with age and the wild foliage that strangled it. I stepped over clumps of nettles and other ugly weeds, tough bracken, and bushes that had given birth to other verdant vandals. I could now see the Gothic facade of the Victorian sandstone edifice – a derelict, neglected affair whose windows were smashed and whose roof was on the verge of caving in. The steps leading up to the door were thick with a solid carpet of long grass and weeds that came up to my knees. Above the doorway was the circular window but with only a few jagged pieces of stained glass left in its frame. The wood of the door was rotten and flimsy. It opened shakily as I pushed it. There, inside the hall, was the same spiral staircase, a few of whose stairs had given way to empty, gaping cavities. I climbed the stairs and observed the dirty and damp wallpaper, which exhibited lighter, cleaner squares where paintings had once hung. There was no doubt in my mind at all now. This was most definitely the beautiful mansion I had visited in the wee small hours of Christmas Day. At the top of the stairs, I saw the open doors that heralded the empty, deserted mess of a drawing room in which I had sat and chatted that Christmas night. The ceiling displayed large spaces that made part of the room above visible. What was this place? And who the hell were the Osbournes? Old Mrs Osbourne and Miss Isabelle? My eyes fixed on the dark brown skeleton in between the hearth and the window. It was the fragile remains of a long-dead fir tree with mouldy and black baubles still hanging from its branches – a Christmas tree, like the one which had been so gaily decorated and whose candles had burned so brightly on Christmas Eve. Hearing a sudden movement behind me on the bare floor, I jerked around nervously, in a second of fear, only to see a huge rat crawl into a cavity in the wall. Then, without warning, a broken shutter dangling from a window crashed onto the floor. The noise echoed throughout the abandoned house. I'd had enough of the place, so I ran down the rickety, creaking stairway and out onto the drive. I tripped over the maze of branches and weeds as I hurriedly made my exit out of the grounds. Back at the wheel of my car, I breathed a deep and long sigh of relief and hit the road back home. I could not wait to leave the place. As soon as I arrived home, I poured myself a large Glenmorangie whisky from the drinks cabinet in my living room. I took a large gulp of the strong stuff from the tea cup I had poured it into, then another. An odd feeling of disbelief, bewilderment, and shock, entwined, had invaded my system, which the strong malt Scotch soon helped dispel. I lay the cup on top of a Christmas card from my first wife, who had remained a friend. It turned into a makeshift coaster so as not to mark the varnish on the antique table. I sat on a sofa in the darkness of the early evening and, as I did so, a nagging seed of curiosity began to grow inside me. I thought about my visit to the Osbournes' at Christmas and was reminded that there were a few things that I had found a bit peculiar but that I had dismissed as mere quaint eccentricities: the candlelight, the black widow's weeds, the antique furniture that looked fairly new, and the general décor of the place. Now, in the cold, logical days of late January, it all seemed extremely odd and certainly out of place.

Several weeks went by and life went on, as it does, into the frosty mornings of February and the snow and ice that followed on the arrival of a late and unusually severe winter. Saracen House had been on my mind a lot, and the more I thought about it, the more curious I became. I decided to phone an antique dealer whom I knew from when I had worked in the business myself. He had a lot of dealings with some of the old buildings on Duncan Avenue through auctions, and I wondered if he might be able to shed any light on the mystery that was Saracen House. The antique shop was situated on a small, narrow alleyway off Hanover Street in the centre of town. Its goods were only just visible through its small window and it was reminiscent of a small house rather than a shop. The dark interior was stuffed to overflowing with a mish-mash of Victorian sideboards, Edwardian bric-a-brac, Chinese wardrobes, and glass cases bursting with faded and worn trinkets. At the end of the long counter stood the bespectacled antique dealer examining a blue and white porcelain figurine. After a few polite words of greeting, I moved on to the subject of Saracen House without divulging the whole story. "Yes, I sold a grandfather clock that had originally come from there."

"So you know the occupants," I said.

"Oh, no, I never met them. The grandfather clock was in the possession of a businessman before I bought and sold it. I remember it well. The poor guy had gone bankrupt and was desperately selling off some of his most prized possessions."

"How awful!" I said.

"Yes, his world fell apart. I heard that he lost his beautiful period house and ended up on some rough council estate." "What a comedown." "It certainly was but I believe a lot of his furniture had originally come from Saracen House."

"Do you know anything about Saracen House?"

"Like what?"

"Well, who lived there. I mean, it`s a derelict pile now, is it not?"

"Yes, it`s such a pity a building like that has been allowed to fall to pieces."

"Have you any idea whom it belongs to?"

"An absentee landlord, one of the Osbournes. Well, a branch of them anyway."

"The Osbournes?"

"Yes, it was the home of the Osbournes since it was built in the early years of the 19th century."

"Do you know who the last inhabitants might have been?"

"Well, the last people to live there were Euphemia Osbourne and her daughter."

"Do you know them?"

"Good god, no! I know of them, through tales my grandparents would tell me."

"What tales would that be?"

"Well, the Osbournes were well known for keeping Christmas in a grand fashion. They were an old family who had lived in the area for hundreds of years. They supported the king during the civil war and were renowned for their magnificently dressed Christmas trees, which would often touch the ceiling. They were, in fact, castigated during the Commonwealth for observing Christmas after it had been banned by Cromwell. My grandfather used to tell me tales about how splendid the colourful festoons and holly boughs were. He would go on about how extravagant the gifts were that the Osbournes presented them with every Christmas."

"Why were they given presents by the Osbournes? Were they related?" I asked.

"The Osbournes held a big annual Christmas party at Saracen House for local children, Mostly for children from poor and deprived backgrounds. That's why my grandparents were familiar with both the Osbournes and the house."

"They sound a generous lot," I said.

"They were but in the end, it was all thrown back in their faces. They were just a bit too charitable to some of the wrong people."

"Why do you say that?"

"Well, the last Mrs Osbourne, in particular, was a good soul who felt that her elevated position in society should not be taken for granted. She thought that it was important to be humble and share some of their privileges with the less fortunate. Christmas was the perfect time to indulge in charitable acts. She was the beloved benefactress of the children's Christmas parties that were once the bright Christmas star of the season for the children of the less well-off. One year, a child came to the party. He had come from a family of petty criminals and he grew up to be a little different. In fact, in adulthood, he turned out to be a worse crook than any of his forefathers. He remembered the Osbournes and Saracen House and in particular the expensive silver and gold artefacts as well as other items of great value that he had seen on his childhood visits to the place."

The antique dealer stopped and took a deep breath.

"One Boxing Day evening, he returned to visit old Mrs Osbourne and her daughter. Now, what was she called again?"

"It wouldn't be Isabelle by any chance?"

"Why, yes, that was it: Miss Isabelle. Well, she and her mother were alone in the house when he called. Being hospitable, as they always were, during the festive season, they invited him in for a refreshment. While they were all sitting in the living room, he suddenly pulled out a shotgun and fired it at both the ladies, shooting Mrs Osbourne dead. He also shot Miss Isabelle, then ransacked the house and made off into the night with a large amount of valuables. Miss Isabelle, nevertheless, survived the terrifying ordeal but before he could be brought to justice, he fled the country and was never seen again. There were rumours that he had become a mercenary in some sort of foreign war and others that he had ended up in South Africa. Whatever happened to him is uncertain but he was definitely never seen again. Well, certainly not in this country."

"And Miss Isabelle?"

"She never married and became a somewhat embittered recluse, suspicious of everything that moved. She allowed no one near the place except for a couple of ageing, well-trusted servants who had worked there for decades. She died a few years after the incident, all alone in that big house."

"And what happened to the house after that?"

"I believe it passed to some distant cousins of the Osbournes. They never inhabited the place and just neglected it. They had a massive auction there some years back when I was just a young assistant in a rather disorganised antique shop, long before I became a dealer myself. I believe that the upkeep of Saracen House became rather exorbitant. It was put on the market for a while but was taken off the market when no one would buy it."

"How long ago was it since old Mrs Osbourne and Miss Isabelle lived at Saracen House?" I asked.

"Well, it was when my grandparents were children. I would say that it must have been about seventy years since the old woman's death. As for Miss Isabelle, she would be dead, I'd say, about sixty years now."

I felt as if I had found the correct pieces that fit into a jigsaw puzzle. The dealer peered at me through the thick lenses of his glasses.

"Can I ask how you know the name of Mrs Osbourne's daughter Isabelle?"

I opened my mouth hesitantly. "Oh, er ... It's ... just that I've heard people mention her in conversation concerning Duncan Avenue."

"Yes, it's a funny sort of place, standing as a lone street in the countryside as it does."

"Yes, of course," I said. "I dropped someone off there on Christmas Eve. I gave them a lift. They'd been to Midnight Mass at the cathedral."

"I went to Midnight Mass at the cathedral myself about five years ago. I never attend church and I`d say that I`m really an atheist but I do enjoy listening to a good choir that can sing excellent, sacred music: Guerrero, de Victorias, and the likes, and there was plenty of that at Midnight Mass. I often attend concerts of classical music, you know."

"Really."

"Yes. It's funny. I remember when I drove back from Midnight Mass that year. There were two ladies on the side of the road just as I turned the sharp corner at Moothill. They flagged down my car. Dressed in black widow's weeds so they were, just like the widows or women in mourning wore in these parts years ago." He chuckled to himself. "A bit quaint, really," he said.

"What did they want?" I asked.

"They wanted me to give them a lift."

"And did you?"

"No, no, as a matter of fact, I didn`t for some reason. I felt somewhat bad about it when I thought about them on Christmas Day. I can`t explain why but there was just something in me that instinctively refused. Clearly, they were two harmless ladies. One looked quite elderly. A mother and daughter, perhaps? I often wonder if anyone gave them a lift on that cold night." He raised his eyebrows and picked up a small figurine. "This came in this morning. It`s 18th-century French. Might it interest you?"

Chapter 5

THE BROKEN NATIVITY SET

The jolly boughs of thick, ever-so-festive, dark green fir needles hung low with heavy, red, velvety baubles encrusted with homely, glistening green diamonds that were, in reality, only highly polished coloured glass. Festively illustrated parcels in a variety of shapes and sizes, tied in ribbons of gold and red and wrapped up so lovingly in a mood of profound Christmas spirit by family members, lay under the tree, whose pungent, special aroma – the official odour of Christmas – filled the living room air. Did the toys come alive after midnight? Did the animals speak as humans did? Was Saint Nicholas flying in the night sky somewhere above our very own home? It was Christmas Eve and everywhere the atmosphere thronged with the peculiar, magical expectation particular only to this holy night. A highly coloured nativity set that I had always had a great affection for sat in the corner of the room on a mat of straw. The three wise men were stunningly attired: Melchior in a scarlet robe and a long, thin gold crown; Caspar in a long purple robe with a black train, his head crowned by an emerald-studded diadem; and the third of the Eastern royal party, Balthazar, with his dark, Arabian complexion under the ermine base of his jagged gold coronet encrusted by rubies, his long, flowing lapis lazuli tunic becoming his regal stature. Their hands were clasped and tightly held their gifts of gold, frankincense, and myrrh in elaborate urns. The night was calm and still and I eagerly awaited Christmas Day with all its delights and surprises.

The perfect stillness was suddenly shattered by a noisy banging on the door and a sudden entrance into the living room of two men and a woman speaking excitedly and sharply with my parents, whose faces reflected an alarming fear. There was movement and the sounds of footsteps running heavily upstairs. Drawers were opened, clothes were quickly taken out of wardrobes, suitcases appeared out of nowhere, and a coat was roughly thrown around me. "We have to go away," said my father.

"Yes, we must leave now," said my mother.

"Can`t we wait till after Christmas?" I asked, confused.

"No, we have to go now," said my father in an agitated state.

As we left the living room to exit the building, I hurriedly ran over to the nativity set and assembled the figurines to take with me.

"No! You can`t take those with you. Come on, we must leave now."

I defiantly grabbed the figure of Balthazar as my father took my hand. However, when we went downstairs into our hallway, I tripped and fell. The figure of Balthazar went flying and crashed onto the floor next to the door. He had been decapitated in the fall and his head and regal body lay separated. My mother pulled me towards the door as I attempted to pick him up, and I only just managed to retrieve his head. Despite my protestations, my mother would not let me stop to pick up his body, which seemed intact despite my having noticed a chip on his hand. A dark-coloured van awaited us as we left through the back entrance to our house. What followed in the hours and days that were then to pass was a whirlwind of frenzied, clandestine activity: new passports, border crossings at night, and then a ferry trip until we finally arrived at our destination, here, which became our home. The events are often very hazy and confused now but I can still see, so vividly, the tree, the presents, and the nativity set in our cosy living room all those years ago. Shortly after our arrival on the island of Great Britain, which on the map seemed too small to hold so many people without them falling off, I was sent to school, only a few hundred yards away from my present dwelling. There, I scraped my knees, got into fights, and lost all trace of a foreign accent. My parents always communicated with me in English at home and, as they made every effort to fit into British life, they even spoke English to each other except in moments of sheer frustration or anger, when they would revert to their native tongue.   This arrangement would often backfire. My mother would say something in English to my father, who would get the totally different end of the stick and go off on an altogether different path. Such little blips did not perturb me in the slightest. Instead, they were, to me, a normal part of domestic life in an otherwise happy home. One problem, although at the time it did not qualify as one, was the fact that I had forgotten how to speak my own language. When I was about thirteen, my mother thought it might be culturally enriching for me to join the local church choir in the weeks approaching Advent. I was reluctant at first and even hostile to her proposal but when I found that membership in the newly formed church football club was open only to boys who could play football and sing – in other words, sing in the choir – I relented, though it all seemed a trifle blackmail-ish to my young mind. The woman in charge of the choir was the organist, a woman of middle age named Gerda MacDonald, who had been born in Berlin but brought up in Nuremberg. It was a wet autumnal evening in mid-November when I ventured out to my first choir practice at the local church hall, a great, draughty barn of an affair attached to a neo-Gothic place of worship, stained black by decades of smoke from chimneys and exhaust fumes from passing automobiles. I had embarked on that first choir practice more than reluctantly and arrived through the heavy old doors of the hall with my lips curled up and my face tripping me. Gerda was full of old, German discipline and, despite greeting us warmly, displayed a no-nonsense tone in her voice. Upon the first sign of discipline starting to crack, she would lower her voice and, in a coldness that would rival the ice on the Baltic Sea and with only a few words of a blizzard, was able to freeze unruliness in its bud. It was not Gerda`s sole aim to teach us the seasonal repertoire for Advent and Christmas worship at the local church. She also intended to educate us in all things festive with a German touch. The war was still a very near and unpleasant memory that hit a raw nerve but Gerda`s Jewish background rendered it acceptable and proper in a period of turmoil and transition that had taken root in post-war Europe. On that first evening of choir practice, we learned Hills of the North Rejoice, and Gerda would not let us go until we had produced a perfect rendering of the first verse. Shouts of

"No! No! No! No!" and "Tommy, will you please sing in key," or "Danny, you are not singing in opera, so don`t behave as if you are" came out of her mouth but all ended well. After the end product had been sung with her approval and satisfaction, she produced a tin foil-covered plate from a cupboard. When she removed the wrinkled tin foil, a powdery sweet seduced our excited tastebuds. She sliced it and put each piece onto an individual plate, which she then passed on to us choir boys. The singing had made us hungry and thirsty. We gobbled the delicious sweet between guzzles of lemonade.

"What`s this?" asked a short, fair-haired child called Roger.

"Why, it`s stollen," Gerda replied, "a German Christmas sweet."

It was a large effort with still plenty on the plate, enough for a second or third helping of it, but when we requested more, Gerda simply pulled the tin foil back over the cake, smiled, and said, "Of course you can have some more ... if you come back next week and sing as well as you did today!"

'More bribery,' I thought.

The week passed with training for the football team on a Saturday morning. Danny Douglas had let in ten goals to the neighbouring school the week before, while I had scored one goal against them, which had made me, temporarily at least, very popular. Poor Danny had gone into hiding for three days while his mother had handed in a letter to school to say he had come down with a winter bug.

Hills of the North Rejoice had been sung just as Gerda had wanted but before we had embarked on any notes, she had looked down at us from the organ loft with a stern glare. It was, post-performance, transformed into a content grin. The next choir practice was minus Raymond Stott, who said he did not want to indulge in such sissyish activities, which ended in his being banned from the football club. The next week, Raymond was queuing up at the church hall door, eager to be part of the choir again. As for Gerda, she kept her promise and gave us who attended two slices of her delicious stollen. Even the crumbs on the tinfoil were gratefully consumed by the choristers.

Gerda announced that if we returned and were again in good voice, she would prepare some marzipan torte for next time.

The following Sunday's rendition of sacred songs was not met with approval. Gerda had struck up the first notes of O Come, O Come Emmanuel, and then we all came in on cue – all except for Micky Jones, who went full speed ahead with gusto into Lo He Comes With Clouds Descending, much to the controlled amusement of the assembled congregants. Needless to say, the much-desired marzipan torte did not materialise.

As we journeyed deeper into Advent and nearer to Christmas, my mind often returned to my early Christmases and the great excitement of the bescheroung when my presents would arrive and I would walk into the living room, with the tinsel adorning the tree for the first time and the candles lit, to retrieve them after the Christkind had delivered and a bell would sound to announce its departure. The Christkind was a blond-haired, mystical, angel-type personage, Saint Nicholas having already left a small gift in my shoes on December 7th. In recent years, Weinachtsmann has proved to be a formidable rival to the Christkind, with his American cultural leanings and likeness to Santa Claus.

Gerda's tales of snowy, freezing Christmases in the Germany of the early 20th century would be brought to life as she veered away from the music and plunged full-heartedly into stories of festive days of old, which, to children who awaited Christmas with great expectation, sounded idyllic. In her tales of Christmas good cheer, the war was forgotten and even Hitler became a nonentity.

As we rehearsed much loved British Christmas carols over and over again until we were all perfect in their rendition, and utterly sick of them at the same time, our credibility as a choir much improved. As we improved, the homemade German baking increased in number, with both cheesecake and kirschtorte making their debut at the end of one choir practice. Often, we returned home full after eating so much. After a particularly gruelling session of attempting to get Hark the Herald Angels Sing to perfection, Gerda announced that because we had advanced so much, she intended to teach us some traditional German carols to perform for a group of German women living in the area who had married British servicemen after their arrival in Germany after the defeat of Nazism. She presented us with sheets of music written in German and announced that in the lead-up to Christmas, we would now have to commit to not only one evening of practice but two. And what if we didn't want to? We knew that our future as minor football stars depended on this and there would also likely be no more delicious cakes if we refused. We overwhelmingly put up our hands in favour of this, which greatly pleased Gerda. The next week, we were rewarded with the best cheesecake I have ever tasted to this day. From there, we went from our over-familiarity with the beloved, traditional British carols into the unknown, mysterious territory of German carols. We warbled our way through the German lyrics of Heiligste Nacht as we peered without guidance onto the carol sheets. Gerda then stopped us and told us to give up trying to read in the meantime. Instead, we were to look at her lips as she sang, then listen, repeat, and remember. Although I could not really recall this carol, some verses seemed to come back to me as if I had already heard them before somewhere in my past early Christmas memories, as did bits and pieces of the language of my primary years, though I could not clearly remember what they meant. This was to prove a rather arduous and trying session, with us having to watch, listen to, and repeat each verse Gerda sang, often up to ten times, and even after that we still didn't get it right and had to watch, listen, and repeat a few more times. However, we did, in the end, manage it. Gerda ended the session late with the words *Menschen Die Ihr Wart Verloren*, which she said meant something like "Humans you who were once lost." She made us repeat it until we had near-perfect pronunciation. Then she put three large pieces of cheesecake onto our plates and poured us lemonade till it almost overflowed from our tumblers. We were to find out that the five words in German were the title of our next work, which we would start in the following practice session.

The days at school that week passed quickly and, as it was now well into December, a chill set in rapidly. Some said that it was going to be another winter like 1947 but it wasn`t to be, which was maybe just as well considering the havoc that it had brought to the country. My star status as a top football player was short-lived and I had been sent off for a foul, which led to the opposing school`s team winning 4 to 1. Star status was brief but proved to be an enjoyable experience. Everyone had been nice to me and wanted to befriend me, if only for a week.

The next choir practice was to be one of the most difficult of the whole season. Clive Franklin repeatedly pronounced German "W's" the English way, despite Gerda`s scolding him a mountain of times. "Please, Clive, for the hundredth time, a German W is pronounced the same as an English V." Clive nodded and then, during the next take, pronounced every German W as a T. "*Humans verloren?*" Gerda gasped in exasperation. "I would certainly say that I am one of them, yes. Now I am completely lost." Rehearsal overran by half an hour, and in case our parents were worried, Gerda asked us to consume that evening's offering – home-baked biscuits – on our journey home.

The Sunday service music seemed a doddle compared to the repertoire for the concert for the German ladies, which loomed high on the horizon. Yet, just like magic, the lyrics and unfamiliar melodies settled into our brains and one morning we woke up and found that we could rattle them off without any bother. Then, the afternoon of the event finally arrived. We all walked with Gerda up to a rather large house on Springfield Street, which had a rather mossy statue of a squirrel in its front garden. We rang the brass doorbell. After a few long minutes, a woman answered and greeted Gerda in German. As we walked inside, away from the cold air, we could hear the loud chatter of people speaking in German from a large room on the left. The same woman handed us a bowl of boiled sweets. We assembled ourselves in a line in front of a large gilded mirror. Gerda stood facing us. As she raised her hands, we began to sing Menshen Dir Wart Verloren. Then, after a pause of a few seconds, we looked at Gerda`s hands as they glided in front of us and we launched into another carol – a routine we repeated until we arrived at the last carol of the repertoire, Stille Nacht. The ladies' eyes looked far away from the room as we sang the first few notes. As Stille Nacht continued, some of the ladies began to hum, then murmur the words, which they soon began to sing softly under their breath. Gradually, more and more of them joined with us until they began to sing as loud as the choir, with them all joining in the singing. We were given rousing applause and soon had plates of kirschtorte and stollen thrust enthusiastically into our grateful hands. As we left the house via the garden with the squirrel statue, Gerda stopped and looked at us with a wide, warm smile. "You have made me very proud today, boys. You sang like true professionals. Well done!"

I did not feel at all hungry due to the large number of cakes I had consumed. When I returned home in the early evening, I had no appetite at all come teatime but I thought it best not to mention this to my mother, who would always get cross if I ruined my appetite between meals by eating too many sweets on my way home from school. I grinned, closed my eyes, and quickly swallowed the fish and cabbage, forkload by forkload, until my plate was more or less empty. I had never liked fish or cabbage in any case, even if I were ravenously hungry, and so had learned to do this down to a T.

My mother and father were interested in how the concert had gone. They were both extremely pleased that things had gone well and that Gerda had gone further and even complimented us. Mother added some salt to her potatoes and then looked over at my father. She began to talk about Gerda. "Her grandmother was a Jew from Berlin who converted and married a Bavarian concert pianist. The whole family was very musical. Some of them were in the Berlin opera. Her brother had some plan to escape but was informed upon and sent to a camp. I believe he's still missing, presumed or more likely definitely dead, though I would never say that to Gerda."

I listened as the foul-tasting cabbage passed down my throat and I felt slightly sick.

"I can't help but think about how lucky we were," said Father. "We had, thank god, friends in high places who staved things off for a while. Many others were not so lucky." Mother sighed and laid her knife on the blue tablecloth. "I often think of Mr and Mrs Weber, the Jehovah's Witnesses who had the sweet shop across the road, and little Gerhart, the crippled boy who used to visit his grandmother in the flat downstairs."

"Yes," said Father. "That morning when the sweet shop's doors remained locked and never reopened, the Webers disappeared in the night. And Gerhart with the laughing face was sent off to some sanatorium or other and died of pneumonia ... they said."

"People often pass through my thoughts. I remember Granddad Fogel pleading to the authorities for some exemption to be made because he had served in the Kaiser's army and had been decorated, and poor old Auntie Gretchen, who wrote a letter to Hitler asking that her hard work for the church and charities be taken into consideration but they came for them regardless, and why? Just because some of our antecedents had come from diverse traditions and had fallen in love? But you can't dwell on the thoughts or you would become overwhelmed with them and they would destroy you, and then the Nazis would have won the true war: the war for our hearts and minds." Mother turned and looked at me. "And don't you go blabbing to Gerda that we've discussed her," she warned in a lowered voice.

"I won't," I said.

I still had not learned the facts behind my parents' low-voiced conversations about the recent past. To me, they were like bits of an unknown jigsaw that floated around in the atmosphere. I caught them but did not have enough pieces to put together and make any kind of picture with.

The concert now over, the Christmas service loomed and my thoughts turned more and more towards the decorating of our family tree on Christmas Eve and the visit of Father Christmas, which the Christkind had now turned into, for, just like me, it had changed cultures over the years and adopted a new country as home.

On the short days leading up to Christmas, Gerda seemed unusually quiet and not her effervescent self. Although she did not display a short temper, there was a heaviness in her hand movements when she conducted and a lacking of enthusiasm in her voice. The carols, due to our prolonged rehearsals, were already fresh in our minds and every descant learned was now perfect. Breathing at the exact time in the delivery was managed with minimum effort. Football was again looking up and I scored two goals at our last match before Christmas, 2 nil to a school in a neighbouring town. What was most unusual to us was that Gerda had forgotten to bring any sort of baking to the last rehearsal before Christmas. On that evening, I made my way out of the hall and into the darkness towards home. After I had walked for about ten minutes, I realised that I had left behind my football boots, so ran back to the hall in the hopes that it was still open. I reached its entrance and saw a light shining through the heavy door and onto the path. Relieved that it was still open, I went into the body of the hall. There, sitting at the desk in its centre, was Gerda with her hands on her head. Before I could say anything, Gerda looked up. "You left your football boots. I was going to drop them off to you on my way home." She then handed me the bag that they were in.

I wondered why she was still sitting there all alone. "Are you alright?" I inquired.

"Yes, I am fine. I apologise for having forgotten to bring you any cakes tonight. It`s just that there has been a lot on my mind."

"A lot on your mind?"

"Yes, I`ve been thinking a lot about my brother lately. I have tried to trace him through various routes, the Red Cross, etcetera, but I always reach a dead end. We spent so many happy Christmases growing up together in Germany."

Without thinking, I opened my mouth and said, "Yes, he was sent to a camp, wasn`t he?" Then, remembering my mother`s warning, I put my hand to my mouth. "I`m sorry, I`m not supposed to say that to you."

A smirk came over Gerda's face that developed into a subdued laugh. "Let's just say I miss him around this time of year."

"I never had any brothers or sisters. An only one I am."

"It was just my brother and me. Mutti was a cheery soul. Father was more silent and strong, though I would say he was most likely silent because he was very shy. Mutti liked to talk to everyone. She was very sociable."

"Who was the eldest: you or your brother? And what was his name?"

"Why, I was the eldest by a few years and his name is Rudi."

"When was the last time you saw him?"

"I have not seen him for many a long year now. My brother tried to arrange an escape for us into Switzerland but one of his friends found out and reported him to the Gestapo. They came one day in spring to our flat, while Father and I were out, and took him and Mutti away. We managed to get to Hamburg, where my father had good friends, and tried to flee the country on one of the many boats in the harbour but none would give us passage except a rather dilapidated ship that was about to leave for Thailand. We jumped on just a few minutes before it set sail. We remained in Bangkok until the end of the war and then came here. Not long after, I met my husband, a crazy professor from the Highlands, and I have to say, the story did turn out happily in the end."

Gerda took a deep breath, smiled, and changed the subject.

"It's Christmas Eve in a few days and I'll be decorating my tree, as I suspect your family will as well."

"Yes, I love when we decorate the tree. It's as if, after so many weeks of waiting, Christmas has finally arrived."

"Some of my tree decorations came with me from Germany, silly little things that I made myself at school. A close German friend gave me a very attractive nativity set when we were reunited after the war. She had found it in some second-hand place and thought it rather unique. It's seen better days but I always put it at the foot of my tree."

"I think it's good that you do that."

"And so, then, I will see you on Christmas morning. Sing well. You won't regret it!"

With that, I left Gerda alone in the hall.

The next couple of days were filled with a Christmas fever and an escapism from the drab post-war atmosphere that still hung over the Britain of the 1940s, when rationing was still in force and the population slowly returned to normal after the trauma and loss of the war years. Shoppers filled the High Street on the 24th in pursuit of what might not normally be available or substitutes if it could not be found. The weather had been mild but there was a sudden drop in temperature and a bitter chill just as Christmas arrived. Like Father Christmas and the Christkind, German and local Christmas traditions merged and borrowed from each other in our home but my parents always insisted that present giving be kept for Christmas Eve. After the tree had been decorated, I put the lone head, the only surviving part of my beloved nativity set, on the sideboard surface and circled it with holly. The evening's alluring uniqueness lived up to my expectations, and as I opened the door of the living room, I was overjoyed to see that my Christmas requests had all been fulfilled. Before I knew it, it was Christmas morning. The Salvation Army had woken up Mum and Dad at 8 a.m. while passing the house with a rousing, if somewhat noisy, rendition of Christians Awake! However, I had slept on. That special feeling of Christmas Day descended on me as I eventually did awake from my sleep. After breakfast, we all got dressed up and ready for the Christmas service, during which I was to sing in the choir. On our way there, we saw several of our neighbours and we all greeted each other cordially with festive salutations ... even the ones we did not particularly care for. It was all part of the magic that was Christmas.

Gerda displayed her best key skills on the ageing organ whose pipes reached up to the heavens in a spire. The vibrant, jubilant tones of Bach's Christmas Oratorio greeted the Christmas congregants as they filled the body of the church until it was standing room only. As the black hands of the clock on the organ loft approached 11 o'clock, Gerda looked down at us in the choir and waved her finger sternly. We then entered into our first carol in good voice, giving as much as our children's vocal cords could. Soon, most of the crystal-clear boys' voices would break, so this would be a swan song for those of us whose voices would become deep and gruff and whose wonderful soprano-singing voices would be lost forever. The service ended with the carol Angels from the Realms of Glory, which, helped along by the congregants, raised the roof of the austere, dark, old building. With the last note sung to perfection, Gerda turned round from the organ, looked down, and smiled excitedly at us with a positive gesture from her fingers. Then, after a couple of silent seconds, she ploughed into Handel's Halleluia Chorus and the smiling, uplifted congregation made its way outside into the nippy mid-day air. We in the choir put on our coats and ran over to our families, eager to get back home to play with our Christmas presents. Some of the boys' parents had not allowed them to open their gifts till after the service. Gerda bid us wait as she finished off the dramatic climax to Handel's masterpiece, which shook the whole church from its foundations to its rafters. Mother and Father looked up towards the loft and then at each other in open approval of Gerda's exceptional playing. She then ran downstairs and gathered the choir boys together, handing us large parcels wrapped in red and green paper. "You have far surpassed my expectations. I never realised you would turn out to be such a well-accomplished choir. Congratulations, boys, and merry Christmas," she said as she affectionately patted us on our heads.

Before she could say any more, Mrs Thomas, the local postmistress, grabbed her by the arm. "Mrs MacDonald, at last I've caught you!" She sounded alarmed

"Caught me?" Gerda asked, somewhat taken aback.

"Yes, there's been a stranger at the post office, asking about your whereabouts!"

"A stranger?"

"Yes, but I kept stum. My lips were sealed and I divulged nothing."

"Well ... erm ... a stranger?" said Gerda, still surprised by the sudden intrusion into her Christmas Day.

"But the problem is, and I had nothing to do with this, nothing at all, he must have gotten news that you were the organist here from someone else, some idle gossip in this town, and, well, he`s..."

"He`s what?"

"He's here today and he`s waiting outside at the door, most probably for you. Oh no, he`s coming back into the church now. Look, here he is!" Mrs Thomas said with a tinge of terror. She stood back as the tall gentleman came running up the aisle towards them.

Gerda opened her mouth and gave out a yell of surprise. The man grabbed her and pulled her towards him in a strong embrace. Gerda burst into tears, then started laughing loudly from her heart.

"My dear, sweet sister! My big sister!" cried the man with tears in his voice.

"Rudi! Rudi! My baby brother. You have found me at last! Thank god! I thought you were dead. Oh, what a lovely Christmas gift!"

"Happy, happy Christmas!" said Rudi joyously.

It was a wonderful sight to see. The remaining congregants in the church smiled happily and wiped tears from their eyes at Gerda`s surprise Christmas present of presents – a display of humanity at its best while they shared in Gerda and Rudi's happiness. The event coloured the remainder of my Christmas Day and that of my parents.

While we ate dinner, Mother and Father discussed the morning. "Gerda was saying that she had a loyal German friend whose family was socialist but managed to keep out of the government`s bad books until the end of the war. She has gone into politics as a profession, after Hitler`s demise. They were reunited briefly after the war," said Mother. "Apparently, she used to live in the same place as us."

"My! What a coincidence," said Father.

* * *

The years have flown by, as have the many decades since that Christmas Day. My boyhood and my clear soprano voice have long deserted me. I am now an elderly man myself, with children and grandchildren. Gerda, a highly talented musician, lived to a great old age and died two weeks short of her hundredth birthday, a few years back. Her husband, Dr Macdonald, a leading academic, lived to be even older than his predeceased wife and passed away at 102 years old. Their house, a large Edwardian affair in Gilbert Park, was later inhabited by her grandson and his family. Gerda had, like many who have come through war, hoarded a lot of items at the house, which ranged from newspapers from the 1940s and 1950s to old letters and faded and damaged Christmas decorations. Her grandson had thought to have a big clear-out and sell a lot of the more desirable pieces of junk as part of a charity jumble, the proceeds of which would go to an organisation that helped people in poor countries have eye operations. On hearing about this event, I thought it might be of interest to go down and have a rummage amongst all the jumble. On one stall was a bundle of dishevelled dollies with bald heads and cracked glass eyes stacked against a pile of faded and wrinkled paperbacks from another age. Right in the middle of them, something caught my attention. It was a rather beautiful and unusual set of the magi which would seem to have once been part of a larger nativity set. I picked it up and inspected it. As I did so, Gerda`s eldest son recognised me and came towards me. "Oh, yes, the old, broken nativity set, a great favourite of my late mother."

"I`ll give you a tenner for it," I said.

"Well, I would have given it away to you for free but since it's a charity jumble, I`ll accept the ten pounds. Very generous of you, thanks!"

"I used to have one that was something like this when I was a kid."

"I think I remember Mum saying that she had been given it by her loyal friend, Brigitte, who went on to become an MP in Bonn. She lived in Erlangen after the war and apparently came across this in a junk shop. Mum liked it but to us, it was just one more piece of old rubbish that clogged up the attic. My mother would be pleased that one of her old choir boys had ended up with it."

"Erlangen. Where we came from originally," I said.

I put the nativity set in a plastic Sainsbury bag and took it home with me.

When I got home, my wife inspected it and commented on how unusual and attractive it was but it was such a pity that the head was missing from the chipped torso of one of the wise men. I took it to place under the Christmas tree and then picked up the head of Balthazar, the Arabian wise man, which sat, as it had done every Christmas for as long I could remember, on the sideboard, encircled by holly. I placed it on the ermine-clad Eastern figure`s body and found it to be the perfect fit. After the many decades that had spanned two different centuries, my own beloved nativity set, lost on that shattered, final Christmas Eve in my natal town, had once again found me.

Chapter 6

A COUNTRY LANE

I saac and Rose Latimer had purchased a rather dreamy, picturesque, 18th-century cottage in the deepest countryside. They hoped to use it primarily for holidays and long weekend breaks. It had only just been renovated before they had bought it, and although quaint and old-fashioned on the outside, it was fitted with the best of amenities inside, allowing the new residents a high degree of comfort. They would drive up from town straight from work on a Friday night, just the two of them. There were no children. Rose, unable to have children, was now in her late forties and had given up all hope of ever being a mother. They had discussed the idea of adoption on several occasions but had never actually gotten round to it, and as both now approached middle age, they had all but given up on the idea. A successful career had brought about a financial security that helped create a fair degree of disposable income to be spent on life's little luxuries. The cottage was one of them, tucked away behind a wall of prickly rose bushes and pine trees. The garden was much loved but just a trifle overgrown, which was how Isaac liked it. He believed it helped bestow the place with some character and an air of warmth. He found well-tended gardens cold and clinical and devoid of any mystery. The building was far from any main road and sat just off a quiet, bushy country lane. Having spent a summer holiday on the island of Sri Lanka back in July, they thought it might be a good idea to utilise the cottage as a Christmas holiday hideaway far away from the shoppers' madness and noisy excess that seemed to have highjacked the festive season.

Rose had always appreciated what lot life had given her and although she felt a sadness in her heart at having never produced any offspring, she had a life philosophy that if you were successful and lucky in many aspects, you should never assume that you should have everything you want from life. You just could not have everything, and that was the rule. She had a happy marriage and was very comfortable in a financial and material sense, and so being childless was just what she had to accept. After all, plenty of couples had children but were forced to live in poverty, with few luxuries.

Isaac shared Rose's philosophy on life and tried to give back a little to the world for having gifted him with success and happiness. He loved his foreign holidays and his quality time at the cottage. They had both resigned themselves to a Darby and Joan lifestyle, totally devoted to each other.

In the approach to Christmas, Rose spent a large chunk of her spare time knitting soft toys for children in refugee camps. These were collected by a local charity that transported them to various centres on the continent. Isaac helped organise Christmas lunches for the homeless, which a host of other volunteers would serve on the big day.

It was on the evening of the 22nd of December, a Friday night, that Rose and Isaac loaded their campervan full of Christmas delights, presents, and decorations, several bottles of Merlot, and a wardrobe of clothes that would last them through the days of Christmas and well into their stay at the cottage. They left immediately after work, as soon as the clock had struck five o'clock. The traffic out of town was exceedingly awful. No sooner had one long queue at the traffic lights come unstuck than another one glued the vehicles to the tarmac for a tedious amount of time.

"It might have been a better plan to have left before dawn tomorrow," said Rose.

"I could have stopped work at noon and then we could have started out earlier and missed the rush hour and the Christmas exit," said Isaac as he adjusted the mirror above his forehead.

"That would not have worked for me. My boss was fairly insistent that we work right up to 5, regardless of Christmas. They were commencing with a small celebration just as I left at 5 sharp," said Rose.

"I suppose it wouldn't have made that much difference. I'd imagine that the roads out of town would be busy for most of today or tomorrow," said Isaac.

"Oh, don't forget to stop and buy a tree at one of the supermarkets."

"I'll wait till we get to one of the villages nearer the cottage. There are always plenty for sale there. minus the manic behaviour and queues at the supermarkets in town."

"That small holding just outside Stoneywood usually has plenty of trees for sale, with some very tall ones, and their prices were very reasonable."

"Okay, we'll try there. We don't want that large a tree, not for the cottage."

"Well, I suppose not. Low roof and doorway."

"Yes, it's the cottage, remember, not the house. Now, a tall tree looks great in the house's living room with the huge bay window."

"Remember that really magnificent-looking one we bought three years back?"

"I certainly do. It touched the ceiling, so it did."

"This is our first Christmas at the cottage. We've never really visited it for much time during the Christmas holidays before."

"No, we haven't but I'm really looking forward to it. A whole two weeks of peace and quiet."

Isaac switched on the radio. Wham's hit Last Christmas was playing. It stopped and was followed by a recent version of Santa Claus Is Coming to Town.

"Can't you put it on something else?" asked Rose.

"Like what? I thought it would put you in a festive mood," said Isaac.

"Yes, I know but I would really prefer something a bit more traditional in the lead-up. That's okay for Boxing Day or the days following it."

Isaac toyed with the car radio and ran along its airwaves until a choir singing Silent Night broke through. He rested the meter onto the frequency and turned up the volume.

"Ah, yes, that's more like it," said Rose contentedly.

"Give me Slade any day!" said Isaac critically.

"I hate Slade. They were everything that was bad about 70s popular culture!" said Rose.

"Nothing quite so festive as good old Noddy Holder belting out Merry Christmas Everybody," said Isaac in response.

Rose turned her head and looked at him, then said,

"And that's one major reason why I thank God it isn't the 1970s." She then returned her ears to the enjoyment of the Gruber carol that had its roots in Austria.

After a two-hour drive through horrendous traffic, they finally branched off the motorway to the side road that led onto Stoneywood. They drove through it, then passed a handwritten sign with "Trees for Sale" scribbled on it. Soon, they came upon a small holding next to a field of cows, where they stopped. They alighted and disappeared for a period of ten or so minutes into the interior of a large shed before resurfacing with a small but perfectly proportioned fir tree that had the aspect of a small child. Isaac opened the boot and placed it in a plastic bin bag.

"This year's Christmas tree," said Rose as she opened the car door as if endowing it with some sort of noble title.

They crawled down the ice-covered roads of the dark, narrow country lanes. The rain from earlier that morning had been followed by a harsh frost that had made the lanes, untouched by the sanders, slippery and difficult to drive on.

"The tires have hardly any grip on these surfaces," Isaac complained. "Thank god we are almost there."

"I thought we could have eaten out tonight at the Hangman's Inn but I don't think we should venture out again," Rose said. "We can have some of that corned beef I bought, along with some potatoes. Then we can put up the tree."

"Good idea," Isaac said. "We can cut down some of the holly in the garden to add a bit more of a festive touch."

"We can always eat out at the Hangman`s Inn another evening," Rose said.

Isaac smiled. "After we`ve been through a week of turkey sandwiches, turkey curry, turkey salad, and turkey fritters, I`m sure we`ll appreciate something from the nosh up at the old Hangman`s," he said.

"Well, it wouldn`t be Christmas without the overdose of turkey variations," said Rose as the campervan swerved on a particularly icy corner next to a bent road sign. She then commented, "That`s such a dangerous bend at the best of times, never mind in wintery weather like tonight`s."

"I know," said Isaac. "But never mind. We`re nearly there."

After they arrived at the cottage, they unpacked everything, then put the food in the fridge and their clothes in the wardrobes. Next, they sat down at the kitchen table and consumed their simple evening meal of corned beef and potatoes, topped with a tablespoonful of Branston pickle, for which Isaac had always had a particular fondness. Rose put on the kettle, took some homemade Christmas pies out of a Tupperware, and made two mugs of tea. Then the couple retired to the relaxing, cosy ambiance of the small living room to watch TV. Tired by a day`s work and the journey from London, they soon both embarked on a snooze far from the entertainment on offer, sleeping as a TV presenter spoke incessantly on some BBC show.

The naked, small fir tree sat in the far corner of the room, feeling neglected.

* * *

Saturday morning exhibited some bashful winter sunshine and the temperature had risen, if only slightly. Rose peered through the kitchen window at the still-white garden as she drank her breakfast coffee from a large black mug.

"I thought we could maybe walk into Little Ham this morning. Either that or go into Stoneywood for a midmorning cappuccino at that little bistro next to the old church."

"Mm…" Isaac said. "Be a bit of healthy exercise as well now that the weather seems to have turned milder."

"You know, this is a world away from London. Just listen," Rose said.

"Listen to what? I can`t hear anything."

"Exactly. There`s total silence outside. How I appreciate that silence after the throng of Christmas shopping in Oxford Street."

"And so few tourists or city weekend ramblers seem to come here."

"Yes, it`s just us, the only city types around," said Rose good-naturedly.

"The thing is, we take the everyday rat race as the norm. It's only when we escape from it that we understand how awful it is," Isaac said.

Rose sighed contentedly. "Yes, I could easily retire here. My days of nights out up the West End are in the past. Been there, done that. Very nice and had a great time but now it's time to move on to something more fulfilling."

"There`s still a tiny part of me that is the fatalistic, hedonistic youth but I can feel that slowly fading away. I`m not ready for a quiet country life yet but I`m heading that way," Isaac said as he clasped his hands over his head.

There was a heavy smell of cooked bacon and percolated coffee in the kitchen which travelled throughout the cottage.

Rose looked at the small fir tree in the room.

"Shall we decorate him now or after we come back from our walk?" she asked.

"I`d rather do it in the late afternoon when it`s starting to get dark," Isaac said. He harboured many little eccentric ideas about tradition and when and where it should be executed. Rose had found this curious at first but gradually, through the years, she had adopted the same mindset.

Stoneywood was a village of only a few shops and a collection of small holdings that punctuated the fields behind the Saxon church. It was a good thirty-minute walk from the cottage along a narrow road lined with ditches. The couple were more than ready for the hot cappuccinos and delicious homemade Bakewell Tart that they purchased in the small bistro on their arrival.

"I brought along that Santa Claus wall decoration. You know, the one with Santa standing outside a snow-decked door with his sack. The one with the white paper festoon that spreads out as you unclip it," Rose said.

"Of course I know it. You've put it up every year for as long as we've been married."

"Yes, I'm really very attached to it. I bought it when I was still at school back in 1963. Christmas just would not be the same without it."

"Mm…" Isaac said, more interested in consuming the homemade tart. He lifted his head, still munching. "We could make our own little holly wreath from all that holly in the garden. There's plenty of it," he said.

"And it's hanging thick with red berries. That's the best kind of holly. So eye-catching," Rose said as she sipped on her coffee.

"A cousin of mine had a florist's shop in Clapham. She made a fortune every year from the sale of holly wreaths. By the time Christmas Day arrived, her hands were raw from the prickly leaves," said Isaac with a tone of pessimism.

Rose put her mug on the table. "Yes, they can be rough on the hands. It might be a better idea to just deck the picture frames and mantelpiece with the branches. I really think that's a better idea, so I do."

"Deck the hall!" Isaac said in a jestful manner.

"Well, it's more a lobby than a hall," Rose said. She grinned and then tensed up her forehead. "We always used to pile thick branches of holly all over the living room and spray it with silver and glitter. Mum had a fondness for the winding crepe festoons that were once so common. We had them strung from the four corners of the living room. My tallest brother, Ben, always stood on the kitchen stool and stretched right up to pin them to the ceiling. We had a very high ceiling when we lived in the terraced house in Clapham. When we moved up to Islington, the rooms were much smaller and the roof much lower, so the holly and festoons never looked so grand. It was a far superior house, mind you, not at all like the draughty old one in Clapham," she said.

"All my childhood Christmases were wonderful, every single one of them. I suppose we romanticise and sentimentalise our old Christmases and our childhood in general," Isaac said.

"I remember the smog and how, due to that, I caught bronchitis a few times during winter. At least that's mostly gone now," Rose said.

"Mmm ... the famous London smog and the public health warnings on TV. I remember, one December, I was confined to bed with whooping cough but recovered enough to enjoy Christmas. It's amazing how much things have advanced even in our lifetime."

A sad wintery sort of sunshine felt fit to come out as the couple walked back to the cottage. It felt much milder and the settled snow began to melt.

At around four thirty in the afternoon, Rose made some hot chocolate. Then she and Isaac proceeded to decorate the small fir tree and place the deep green holly, covered in attractive red berries, on various objects in the living room. Darkness had fallen and when the Christmas tree lights were switched on, they gave a colourful and welcoming air to the place. The final part of the decorating ritual came when Rose picked up two drawing pins and put her beloved Santa Claus picture on the wall next to the door. Its white papered snow fanned out from the flat illustration. Everything looked in place, perfect and ready for Christmas.

Isaac picked up a copy of the local newspaper, which they had bought on their way back from Stoneywood.

"According to the forecast, it's going to snow heavily tomorrow evening."

"A true white Christmas. And us all cosily sheltered in here. I love white Christmases but we seem to get them a lot less often these days," Rose said.

"Mmm, they can have their pros ... and cons," Isaac said with mixed feelings of positivity and negativity.

Rose relaxed farther back into an armchair, her head deeply embedded in a large velvet cushion. "I often wonder how it would have been," she said.

"How what would have been?"

"Well ... if we had children. How Christmas would have been if we had had children. I often think how it would have been on Christmas morning ... our children opening their presents."

Isaac was silent for a few seconds. "Well, we don`t have any children. We just have to accept that. If you dwell on it, you`ll only get upset. We have passed that stage now. Just thank god that we are healthy and have each other and that it's Christmas."

"You`re right, I suppose."

"Look at this."

"What?"

"There`s an advert for a candlelight Christmas concert in the village square in Little Ham tomorrow. Christmas Eve," Isaac said.

"Yes, that sounds very festive."

"Hot chestnuts and mulled wine on sale."

"Perfect. That`s a must. I can have some mulled wine and you can drive!" Rose said.

"Or, rather, you drive and I`ll drink some mulled wine!" Isaac replied.

"Whatever. If you're that desperate for a drink, of course I'll drive," Rose said as she teased her husband.

Isaac laughed "Oh! And who got so drunk at the French class`s Christmas party two years ago that she threw up in the kitch..."

Rose cut off Isaac before he could finish his sentence.

"I was only sick because someone had put far too much spirits in the hot punch!" she said.

"Oh, really? Was that the excuse, sorry, reason?"

"Yes it was, actually, and anyway, you know I like quiet, restful Christmases."

"Yes, okay, so tomorrow evening's schedule will start with the Christmas concert at 7:30 in Little Ham," Isaac said, getting back to the topic of Christmas Eve.

"Confirmed," Rose said happily.

"Now, how about something to eat? It's nearly 6 o 'clock and I'm starving." Isaac said as he rose from the sofa.

"I'll just hoover the carpet. Look at the bits of tinsel and pine needles all over it. You can take the vegetables out of the freezer," Rose said.

* * *

Rose awoke early on the morning of Christmas Eve to take Isaac's present out of the camper van, wrap it up, and hide it behind a cabinet in the shed before he awoke. He had already hidden hers – a highly unusual necklace that he had bought from a curious little shop in Colombo while on holiday in Sri Lanka earlier that year. She had eyed it up on the few occasions that they had shopped there. He had returned later in the holiday and bought it but Rose herself had returned and had been most disappointed to find that it was no longer on sale.

After breakfast, Isaac took the turkey out of the small freezer which they kept in a tiny box room next to the kitchen. It would take a long time to defrost. He looked out of the living room window. It still looked rather mild despite what the forecast said in the newspaper. Rose rushed around, dusting here and there, over sideboards, table surfaces, and the few ornaments with which they had adorned the place in an attempt to make it more homely. Then they both put on their thick winter coats and scarves and walked once more along the narrow country lanes lined with hedges and overgrown foliage into the village of Stoneywood for a cappuccino at the small cafe which they so liked. They sat snuggled on a leather sofa in front of a fireplace.

"It's Christmas Eve so I`m going to have a couple of those mince pies in the glass case over there," Rose said.

"I think that I might as well but then there`s always the big question when it comes to ordering mince pies."

"And what`s that?" Rose asked.

"Well, I thought that would be obvious. Will they taste as good as yours?"

"Yes, very droll. I like it."

"You know, if we're going to have some mulled wine tonight, why don`t we both walk to Little Ham? Then there`s no issue with driving," Isaac suggested.

"Well, that`s one option but the downside is, if we do that then we`ll both have to walk all the way back."

"Mmm ... And it is a bit of a walk."

"Yes, a good forty minutes or three-quarters of an hour. I think it's best to drive. You can take the wheel when we go and I`ll drive back. I don`t mind not having any mulled wine. I`ve got a bottle at the cottage that I bought in Marks and Spencer. I can have some when we arrive back from Little Ham," Rose said. She looked Isaac in the eye. It was a look he recognised, and he knew what was coming.

"I`m just thinking," she continued. "It's such a pity that we don't even have any nephews or nieces. You being an only one with no siblings and Ben having been married briefly four times and no issue, and even if he had children we would never see them in that he lives in California."

"I know. Often, childless couples become close to their siblings' children, But hey! You`re on the way to getting yourself upset again."

"Well, it's my fault that we couldn`t have any offspring."

"Look, I`ve told you before, we have each other and now that`s all that matters. Some things were just never meant to be."

Rose finished off the last piece of the mince pie. "You know, in answer to what you asked me earlier: I much prefer my own homemade mince pies to these."

* * *

The village square in Little Ham was decked in simple coloured bulbs with a large, rather grand star that hung over its centre. A large fir tree stood underneath. It was sparsely lit, with several of its lights having fused.

A small makeshift stage had been erected on its left-hand side with a slightly lopsided Christmas tree on its platform.

Isaac had driven over, and Rose was to drive on the return journey, as she had said she would. They parked the campervan in a side street at the back of the square. The first sounds from the concert were audible as they alighted from the van and onto the pavement. A dazzling sight met them as they entered the square, which was slowly filling up with people. Angels with bright gold wings, Santas in bright red, elves in deep green, and vocalists in shiny gold suits were everywhere as a woman in her thirties, dressed like a Christmas tree, belted out an early 1960s Phil Spector Christmas song. She was followed by a group of school children who sang the Rocking Carol and exuded a most sober expression as they performed. They obviously took the whole thing most seriously. A short, middle-aged lady with Rudolph earrings dangling from her ears handed two tickets to Isaac and Rose in exchange for a ten-pound note.

"Roasted chestnuts, mince pies, and one glass of mulled are included in the charge. Please present them at the refreshments stall," she said.

"You can drink my mulled wine," Rose said.

"And you can have my mince pie in reward for your little sacrifice," Isaac replied.

The golden-clad vocalists stepped up to the microphone and embarked on a medley of Christmas hits from the 1970s that were popularised by Mud, Slade, Shaking Stevens, and Wizzard, respectively. Isaac was in his element and even sang along to a couple of them. Rose watched him from the corner of her eye. She smiled but failed to comment.

'It's nice to see him enjoying himself,' she thought.

At the interval, everyone queued at the small refreshments stall. Rose consumed her mince pie quickly. No sooner had she done so than Isaac handed his to her. The pies were obviously homemade and baked in different homes. They were all very unique in size, pastry, colouring, and flavour.

"Just what I had expected. These don't come up to the same standard as my own home-baked," Rose said.

"I never expected them to!" Isaac said.

The concert resumed with the same woman who had earlier performed the Phil Spector number. This time, gave a rendering of White Christmas. Some primary school children dressed in biblical robes and headdresses then took to the stage and put on a mini nativity play, at the end of which the school choir joined them to sing Silent Night. A couple of amateur actors from the local rural dramatic society gave everyone a performance of an extract from It's a Wonderful Life, with one in the role of George Bailey and another as the guardian angel. It ended with all the entertainers and the audience joining together in the singing of Hark! The Herald Angels Sing. Everyone then began to leave with a festive feeling in their bones. Just as they did so, the temperature dropped quickly and snow started to fall heavily onto Little Ham. Rose and Isaac pulled their scarves up to their throats and dug their hands into the pockets of their thermal jackets. They had driven for ten minutes and were in the middle of a narrow country road. "It was all very lovely. A bit impromptu but all very heartfelt," Rose said.

"The concert was a genuine community effort. Not exactly Westminster Abbey but that's what I liked about it all. So very much love put into it and free of all pretensions," Isaac said.

Suddenly, the snowfall turned into an unexpected wild blizzard which began to make it nigh impossible to see the road in front, despite the windscreen wipers moving frantically from side to side. The campervan crawled slowly along the road. Rose looked worried.

"Maybe it wasn't such a good idea to venture out tonight. I can't believe how suddenly all this started," she said.

Isaac peered through the windscreen. "Maybe we should have stayed at the cottage and watched all the festive fare on the TV," he said.

"Well, it's too late to do that now. We're in the middle of all this, like it or not."

"It's going to take ages to get back at this speed."

"Just be patient and be glad that there's hardly any traffic on the roads."

They passed the Hangman's Inn, its roof now covered in thick white snow and the building barely visible from the campervan window. The place looked deserted and devoid of any festive revellers.

Just as they turned at the blind corner next to the bent road sign, which had been the result of a car accident some years previous, the campervan skidded on a thick sheet of ice that had formed on the road's surface. Rose managed to manoeuvre the vehicle back onto the adjoining country lane that led to their cottage. As she crept slowly along the lane through the sheer darkness and blinding snowfall, a woman wearing a white headscarf and a fawn coat seemed to jump from out of the roadside bushes. She was in a highly distraught state and, screaming and wailing, banged her fists against the widows. Feeling somewhat stunned by the sheer unexpectedness of this, Isaac and Rose looked at each other in horror.

"What's she saying?" Isaac asked.

"What on earth has happened?"

"Open the window, quickly," Isaac said.

"What's wrong? What is the problem?" Rose asked nervously as the woman pushed her head frantically towards her as Rose pulled down the window. Rose noticed that she had clear blue eyes and a gash

on her forehead, graced by a couple of thick black curls that protruded
from the white headscarf tied tightly around her throat.

"It's my baby! Please help my baby!" she screamed at the top of
her voice. "Please, I beg you, save my baby's life! For god's sake,
please!"

Isaac undid his seat belt and jumped hastily out of the van.

"Now calm down, please. What's the problem and how can I
help you?"

With tears pouring out of her eyes and her body shivering with
terror, she tried to speak clearly.

Rose jumped out of the van and put her arms around the woman
in an effort to comfort her.

"It's my little boy! There's been an accident! Please, you must
come quickly! This way, over there!" she said as she beckoned Isaac and
Rose over to an opening in the bushes. On a snow-covered slope below
lay a badly damaged car which would seem to have been in an accident.
The woman began yelling and screaming once again. Isaac tried to keep
his cool as he made his way down the slope, which he did with
difficulty. Rose watched in concern. Isaac drew closer to the car and
saw, at the steering wheel, a man in his forties with a black beard and
dark hair hanging over his face, which was pressed against the
dashboard and covered in blood. Isaac checked his breathing and felt
his pulse.

"The car's a total right off," Rose said. "He's already dead,"
shouted Isaac.

In the passenger seat, with a thick gash in her head, slumped
against the windscreen, was a woman, maybe in her thirties, who
appeared to be vaguely familiar. Did he know her?

He touched her brow and then her mouth to see if she was
breathing. Then he felt her pulse as well. She, too, was dead.

From the back seat of the car came a whimpering little noise and
then the sound of a baby's cry. Isaac unstrapped the baby and carried
it carefully over to Rose, who was now standing near the damaged car.
Rose cradled the baby in her arms and hugged it.

"He seems to be unharmed, thank god. Poor little soul. Doesn't he look so sweet?" Rose said, then turned to talk to his distraught mother, glad to tell her that her baby seemed unharmed. However, when she turned round, the woman was no longer there. Mystified at her disappearance, Rose moved forward to inspect the two bodies in the car.

"Look, Isaac, that woman!"

"Yes, there's something familiar."

"Look at the gash on the forehead! The white headscarf!"

"And the black curls! But..."

They looked at each other with expressions of total disbelief. What was happening?

Isaac climbed back onto the road and peered both left and right through the deluge of snow but there was no sign of her. He looked at the white ground. The woman had left no footprints. With an enigmatic intensity in his eyes, he walked back towards Rose.

"The dead woman in the car. She's the woman who flagged us down. This must be her baby," he said.

"Yes," Rose said. "Her baby boy."

"We must call the police and the ambulance. They must be informed, though there's not much they can do now," Isaac added.

Rose shook her head. "No, those poor souls are beyond help now, and that poor baby. How absolutely awful."

Both in a state of shock, they were silent for some minutes. Then they carried the baby back to the shelter of the van as the snow continued to fall heavily. When they had driven less than a hundred yards, they heard a violent explosion. They turned to look behind them and saw the car go up in flames.

"Thank god we got him out in time!" gasped Rose.

* * *

The baby boy whom Isaac and Rose had rescued was the son of the couple killed in the accident. He had no other siblings or close relatives, and so they adopted him and gave him the name of Noel Emmanuel because they had rescued him on Christmas Eve. Isaac and Rose were to become exemplary parents and gave the child much love. As he grew older, he became filled with love. People gravitated towards him because of this. He would have many friends and fall in love and have children whom he also showered with much love, which made them extremely happy and balanced people. It was as if the light of Christmas shone in him and those he encountered.

Printed in Great Britain
by Amazon

32891470R00071